It was hard to sit in his saddle because there was barely an area of his body that had not been scraped or bruised. He had been dragged slowly at the end of a rope, and he was in bad shape.

As he rode he flexed the fingers of his right hand. They were stiffening. Fear came in a rush—what gunspeed would he have now? Would he survive the showdown with the man who'd killed his family?

He had three deaths to avenge.

One man to kill.

One gun to help him.

GUN SHY

by
Les Savage, Jr.
and
Dudley Dean

WILDSIDE PRESS

Chapter One

THERE WERE GUNSHOTS in Table Rock. The town was half a mile away but the sound brought Gordon Conners to his feet, trembling. He stood on top of the huge overhanging rock that gave the town its name. From the flat-topped vantage he could see the buildings far below— the gray shafthouses and black smokestacks of the coal mine, the gleaming spiderweb of railroad tracks, the flimsy tarpaper shacks and false-fronted frames clinging precariously to the steep streets. He could see a crowd on Main, in front of one of the saloons, but it was too far away to make out what they were doing. He was still trembling and dry-mouthed. It was what the sound of gunfire always did to him.

Shading his eyes he saw a rider leave the outskirts of town and take the trail leading to the rock. He recognized a paint horse and realized it was probably Opal Bayard. She was the niece of Roland Bayard, one of the few friends Gordon's father had in town. Opal knew how much time Gordon spent on the rock, dreaming a young man's dreams. His hazel eyes watched the approaching rider. The eyes changed color as the light changed, turned black by the shadow of his thin hand. His face was thin too, almost fragile, topped by shaggy black hair that hadn't felt scissors for six months.

Opal forced the laboring paint up the steep trail till it snorted with the effort. She was eighteen—two years younger than Gordon—a girl with sun-colored hair and a woman's shape to her body that even the yards of her long riding skirt couldn't hide. Gordon moistened his lips. He wished he wasn't so abashed with girls. The

5

Bayards were the richest family in Table Rock, and Opal had been educated in a St. Louis Academy. It always made him feel like he was standing up before a schoolmarm. But it was more than that. It all seemed tied up with his daydreaming, his fear of guns, the things in him that didn't belong to a farmer's son. At twenty, a man should know more about women.

"Gordon," Opal called. "Gordon—it's your father. They think he rustled some Crazy Moon beef."

He started running to meet her. "That shooting— they're not—"

"No, no—just some Crazy Moon cowhands. They've been drinking in the saloon—working themselves up to this. I was in Uncle's office when I heard . . . Gordon, they're going after your father!"

It kicked the wind out of him. It made his voice sound thick and strange. "Opal—give me your horse. You've got to."

She pulled the paint to a stop as he reached her. She looked at him for an instant, her lips parted, as though to say something. Then she stepped down. He uncinched the clumsy sidesaddle, jumped on the paint bareback. He gave a last look at the girl, then wheeled the paint and broke into a gallop down the trail. He saw a dozen riders leave Table Rock. They passed the spot where the trail met the road long before he reached it. There were some stragglers still coming from town. As Gordon got to the road a man on a roan passed, carrying a rifle across his saddlebow. Then a pair of younger men. One was Billy Halleck, a big redhead, two years older than Gordon. His front teeth had already been chipped in a dozen brawls and they showed in a wicked grin as he saw Gordon. He hauled his horse to a halt.

"Better stay here, Gordon," Halleck said, winking at his companion. "There's liable to be some shootin' when they catch your pa. You wouldn't want to hear any shootin', would you?"

Halleck laughed and kicked his horse, plunging on down the road.

The man with Halleck held in his horse, eying Gordon. The man, a stranger, gave Gordon a long look out of pale eyes. His face was dark, long, his mustache thin. He wore a waist-length blanket coat, the lashes dangling. At his belt was a black-handled gun.

6

"So you're the kid they say is gun shy," the man said. "I feel sorry for you. Gun shy—in country like this."

Shaking his head the man pushed his sorrel on down the road where Billy Halleck was waiting for him.

Gordon sat his horse, this talk of guns turning him sick with fear. And the sickness grew when he remembered what Halleck had said: "There's liable to be some shootin' when they catch your pa." He tried to swallow and it seemed his throat was swollen with fear. He knew how bad the feeling was among the cattlemen. They had been nearly driven to the wall by rustling this last year. Not a month ago a pair of saddle bums had been caught with a running iron down near Green River and had been lynched.

The road followed the pass through the foothills into Stirrup Basin beyond. It was the route the Crazy Moon riders had taken. There was still a faint haze of dust that marked their passage. He knew he could never hope to catch them that way. By heading directly over the ridge he could cut off three miles. It was a horse-killing route but the only way he could reach home ahead of the others.

He sent the paint plunging across the road and up the steep rocky slope. The tall, yellow rabbitbrush whipped against the horse's legs. There was a throbbing ache between Gordon's shoulders. It made him realize the muscles had been knotted up ever since leaving the rock, rigid with the tension of anticipating more shots.

It filled him with helpless fury. There was nothing he could do about it. One gunshot and he was spooked for the rest of the day. It had been with him all his life. His father had told him he was no better than a gun shy horse—and had tried to cure him the way he would a horse. When the whippings and the tricks and the threats and the briberies had failed, his father had taken Gordon to a doctor. The doctor could find nothing wrong. He said the boy would grow out of it. That had been a long time ago.

Gordon reached the rust-colored rimrock, a sandstone ledge that had been scoured by the wind and the rain till its countless miniature caverns gave it a weird moth-eaten look. The hot breeze brought him the smell of the sulphur springs on his flank.

Stirrup Basin spread below him—the sage flats and the grama meadows and the green band of willows where

7

Sulphur Creek wound through the wastes to the point where the house and corrals had been built. Gordon's father, Bob Conners, had brought his family here a few months before, and had filed on a homestead.

Crossing the creek, Gordon looked to his right and saw the first riders appearing in the pass. He had gotten ahead of them. The paint waded belly-deep across the creek and lunged into the buckbrush of the bottoms. Gordon headed up the dry wash that led to the house. He fought to halt his horse as he caught sight of a bunch of cattle ahead of him, held by a pair of riders. One of the men was enormously tall, with a longhorn mustache and a hard hat. Gordon recognized Tom Union, one of the Crazy Moon hands.

He realized that this must be where they had found the rustled cattle. One rider must have gone back for the rest of the Crazy Moon crew while Union and the second man held the evidence in the wash.

Union shouted when he saw Gordon and put spurs to his horse. Gordon drove the paint up out of the wash and headed in a dead run toward the cottonwood grove. He couldn't believe his pa had brought those cattle here. His pa wasn't the kind to rustle. It had to be some kind of mistake. Some kind of mixup.

As he ran into the grove he saw Union appear at the edge of the wash. The man pulled to a halt, silhouetted there, evidently not wanting to get any closer to the house till he had the rest of the crew with him.

Through the cottonwoods Gordon could see the dugout. Bob Conners had made a single room by cutting a niche deep into a head-high hummock of land, so all they had to put up was the sod-brick front wall and the roof. Gordon knew that at this time of day his father would be ploughing in the fields beyond the house. It was why he wouldn't know about the cattle being held in the wash. Gordon galloped the paint past the house and up the low ridge.

He saw his father in the field. Bob Conners had halted his mule and his bull-tongue plough. He had one hand shading his eyes and was staring at the yellow cloud of dust the riders had lifted in the pass. When he saw Gordon on the paint he walked across the furrows toward him. Bob Conners was a tall man, dusty, stooped with the ague and with a lifetime of labor. He had knobby joints, and a ploughman's callouses made horny ridges on his immense hands.

"So you come home, tail between your legs," he said disgustedly. "Maybe now you'll stand up like a man and shoot a gun—"

Gordon, trying to catch his breath, made an impatient gesture. He and his father had quarreled this morning. Quarreled because Gordon wouldn't take a rifle and go into the hills after deer.

"Pa, you got to get away," Gordon said. "They're comin' to string you up. Say you rustled some Crazy Moon stuff. I saw it down there in the wash."

Conners reached the top of the ridge, breathing heavily. He stared at Gordon, the blood draining from his face, and then looked again toward the yellow dust hanging over the pass. Gordon heard the door of the dugout creak on its rawhide hinges. He turned to see his mother coming out, drawn by the sound of his horse, or their voices. Sarah Conners was a bent woman, turned old before her time by her frontier labors. Her hands were corded and dirty—and one of them was held at her throat in a frightened way. Her voice sounded strained.

"What is it, Bob?"

Bob Conners had Gordon's same hazelnut eyes that seemed to change color according to the light. They had turned a shining green in the bright afternoon sun, as he continued to stare toward the pass.

"Maybe we're about to pay a debt, Sarah," he said. "It's been a long time acomin'. Git inside, both of you."

He grabbed Gordon's arm in a grip that hurt, pulling him off the paint and turning him down the low ridge. Gordon followed his mother into the dugout. It smelled of wet earth and the floor was still gluey from the water that had seeped through the sod roof during the last rain. Gordon's father pulled the door shut and barred it. He crossed the room to take his big Sharps down from its antler rack over the fireplace. Gordon had never seen anything spook his pa, or hurry him. He spoke as deliberately as he moved.

"Now, you listen to me. If they start shooting, you git out the back way. Both of you. Hear me, Gordon? You git your ma to Roland Bayard's—"

"I'm agoin' to stand with you," Sarah said. "All we got to do is wait for Sheriff Simms."

9

"Simms won't come," Conners said. "You know how they got him sewed up in this county."

"It don't matter," Gordon said. "Ma's right. We can't leave you."

"If you're bound determined to look so brave, you better have a gun," Conners said. Gordon couldn't tell if it was sarcasm in his father's voice or not. His father held the Sharps out abruptly. Gordon stood as if frozen. It was what his father had done earlier in the day, when they quarreled. Gordon took a step back, away from the rifle. He couldn't help it. He saw the bitter shape come to the older man's lips.

"Pa," Sarah said. "When are you agoin' to accept the fact Providence didn't give us a boy like the rest?"

Conners turned his back. He began taking some linen-cased cartridges out of the box, moving so slow Gordon thought he was counting them.

"It may be they'll follow you to Bayard's," Conners said. "They know him'n me were friends. If Bayard can't protect you—you got one chance left. Find Blackhorn."

Gordon stared at his father. It was the first time he had heard Blackhorn's name mentioned in ten years. The man was a legendary figure to Gordon. Someone he had never seen. Gordon never knew whether Blackhorn was Bob Conners' closest friend or his worst enemy. Something dark had happened between them a long time ago, something Gordon had never been told.

"Pa," Sarah said. "Why Blackhorn? This ain't got nothing to do with that."

"How do you know?" Bob Conners' face looked sunken, haunted. His eyes made a catlike glow in the dim light from the bottle window. The earth began to tremble beneath their feet and Gordon knew it was the riders approaching. Conners made a motion toward the back door. "Open it, boy."

Not many dugouts had back doors. It was one of the strange quirks in his father that Gordon had never fathomed. Bob Conners never had a house with only one way out. He had cut his room into the hummock, instead of a sidehill, so that he could dig a rear passage that opened out on the opposite side of the hump of land. Gordon unbarred the waist-high door. It scraped wet clay from the floor as he pulled it open. He realized the earth had stopped trembling.

"Bob Conners!"

10

The voice was muffled, hollow, coming from some distance outside. Gordon figured the riders had halted among the cover of trees. The breechblock made a soft click as Conners opened the action of the Sharps, shoving one of the cartridges home. Sarah made a sighing sound.

"Come out, Conners," the man called again. Gordon recognized the heavy voice of Rodger MacLane, the Crazy Moon owner. Conners went to the window, calling outside.

"We can talk from here."

"Ain't no talking to do," MacLane answered. "Tom Union and two other riders o' mine found some of my beef in your draw. You done a helluva sloppy job changing my Crazy Moon to your Stirrup."

"If I'd blotted your brand do you think I'd be fool enough to leave the beef around for anybody to stumble across?"

"We didn't come to argue, Conners. You got a minute to come out."

"What for?"

"A trial," MacLane answered.

"The judge with you?"

"We got enough men for a jury."

"A Crazy Moon jury. That'll make sure of a hangin'."

"There's more than Crazy Moon men here, Conners. The town's fed up with men like you. I've lost half a thousand head of beef in four months. Anvil's lost cows. So has Seventy-Seven. We're fed up with men like you. If the law won't stop it we will. That minute's just about up."

"There's my woman and boy in here."

"You can't call Gordon a boy any more. Have you got anything to prove he wasn't in on the rustling?"

"That's what I thought," Conners muttered. He glanced at his wife and son. "Git in that tunnel—both of you."

Gordon looked at the big gun in his father's hands. If it came to a shooting . . . a tremor ran through him. He couldn't control it.

"Ma," he said. "You go on."

"You go with her," Conners said. "Do as I say, boy, or I'll meet you in hell with a horsewhip."

MacLane called from outside. "Your last chance, Conners."

Conners didn't answer. He sent his son a savage glance.

Gordon's palms were clammy.

"I can't go," he said. "Ma, you git out. Please. You git out."

There was a smash of a shot. The bullet cracked the door and thudded into the clay behind Gordon. Conners smashed the bottles out of the narrow window with his rifle butt.

"Git out," he shouted. "Sarah—git out!"

He fired through the opening. The shot made a roar in the room. The shock of it seemed to shake Gordon's whole body. It was answered from outside by a barrage. Bullets cracked through the door, smashed through the broken bottles of the window. The deafening sound sent a senseless panic through Gordon. He saw his father clap his hands to his face and stagger backward. Then Gordon couldn't see any more. He couldn't see or think. His only sensation was the noise, the shattering crash of guns, the roar in his ears that was so close to pain and yet not a pain.

He found himself in the tunnel, stooped over, clawing his way through like some wild animal in a trap. He didn't know how he had gotten there. He couldn't remember leaving the room. He was halfway through the narrow tunnel when he realized he was alone. His mother had not followed. There was no more shooting.

The shots still seemed to echo through the corridors of his mind, but he realized it was inside, some trick of his brain. The shooting had stopped. He crouched against the wall, holding his head, shaking violently.

"Ma," he called. "Ma. . . ."

There was no answer. He wanted to run. He knew the shooting would begin again. He had to run. Hating himself, hating his weakness, he forced himself to turn back. He crawled along the tunnel. He was drenched with sweat, suffocated by his panic. He came out into the room, fighting for control. His father lay in the shambles below the broken window, hands still held against his bloody face. His mother lay huddled in the corner against the wall. Gordon went to one knee beside her. She had been hit twice. He saw that she was dead.

"Gordon . . ." It came from Bob Conners. He still had one hand held blindly to his smashed face. Gordon saw that he had been hit in the body too. His chest was soaked with blood. He was fumbling for something beneath his shirt, pulling out a thin wallet. He made a rattling sound

12

in his throat. "Blackhorn . . . last I heard . . . up in the Wind Rivers somewhere—near South Pass City . . . the Indians will know . . ."

Gordon realized he would have been lying beside his father and mother if he hadn't thrown himself into the tunnel during the firing. A sense of guilt swept him. He saw that his father meant him to take the wallet. It was wet with blood, in his hand. A convulsion shook Conners. He made a choking sound, clawed feebly at Gordon's arm. He sagged back. The hand slid off his wrecked face.

"Conners," MacLane called from outside. "You've killed one of my men. You come out or we come in!"

Gordon stared at his father. His brain seemed numb. He couldn't feel anything. His father was dead. There was something wrong with him. His father was dead and his mother was dead and he couldn't feel anything. He looked at the Sharps his father had dropped. He reached out. He made a broken sound. He couldn't pick it up.

The shooting started again.

He fought it for a moment. The effort brought a sob from him. Then he lost control. He turned and ran. He couldn't help himself. It was inside his head again, the sound, the roar, the crashing of guns, louder than reality, engulfing him with a primitive terror. He was in the tunnel, his head scraping dank clay from the low roof. He was at the other end, clawing to unbar the door. He was so panicked that he didn't even wait to see if anybody was outside.

He plunged into the brush that screened the door. The low ridge of earth hid him from the riders as he ran for the creek. Nobody knew about the back way out and apparently the fight had kept them all around front.

Gordon reached the river, his shirt half torn off by the clawing brush. He was still wild with panic. He turned downstream in the shallows of the river. He ran like an animal.

Chapter Two

ROLAND BAYARD'S HOUSE was two miles across the basin from the Conners' homestead. Gordon knew he would have headed that way even if his father hadn't told him to. Bayard was the only one he could turn to in Table Rock.

The man had been a close friend of Bob Conners in the past. Gordon had been a baby, too young to remember, and his folks had never talked much about it. But when the family was in debt or sick or up against it in any way, it seemed to Gordon that his mother was always telling his father to "look up Roland, he'll help you."

Gordon's father hadn't done it till this year, only a few months ago, when things had turned so bad that they didn't even have the fare to Table Rock, and had to walk the last hundred miles from Laramie. Bayard was division superintendent for the railroad in Table Rock. He had taken the day off to help, going with Conners to file on a homestead, obtaining credit for him at the store for the plough and stock and seed and supplies he would need. Bayard had come out to the homestead several times after that. Gordon had thought it was downright human for such an elegant man to sit in a dirt room and drink chicory coffee with his old friend. He had even invited the Conners family up to his place. It was a big house, whipsawed lumber shipped from a Laramie mill, tall hip roof to shed the Wyoming snow, a long gallery of smooth round stones cemented with grout.

Gordon would never know how he reached the place that night. He guessed he must have run all the way from the dugout. He stumbled in through the grove of poplars. A whiskey jack scolded him from the branches and the trees shed their feathery tufts on him like a snowfall. He dropped to his knees and sagged across the stone steps, so spent he couldn't move. He ached all over. It hurt so much to breathe he thought he was going to cry.

The Bayards must have heard him from inside, sobbing for breath. The door was open and a yellow path of light fell across his dirty, bleeding figure sprawled on the steps.

He saw figures silhouetted in the doorway. Curiously enough it wasn't Roland Bayard who first crossed the porch to him. It was a gaunt man in a cranberry-red fustian. Gordon had met him here once before. He was Adam Chaney, Bayard's brother-in-law. Although he looked anything but a cattleman he ran a few cows west of town in the Double X iron. Gordon had gotten the impression he was some sort of family black sheep. His long face had a yellow tinge, the same ague-color Gordon

14

had seen in so many bottomlanders along the Missouri.

"Pa," Gordon gasped. "Pa. Crazy Moon—out there. Saw 'em in the draw. He didn't do it—"

Roland Bayard crossed the porch after Chaney, saying sharply, "Snap out of it, Gordon. Settle down. I never saw a kid so spooked."

"Give him a chance, Roland," Chaney said. He knelt beside Gordon, gripping his arm. He had a strange voice, almost like an echo. "Settle down now, Gordon. You're with friends. You're safe."

"They shot," Gordon gasped. "All that shooting—"

Bayard made an impatient sound. He was a big man, moleskin trousers the color of sassafras, a steel pen coat that must have cost a hundred dollars. Gordon was aware of Chaney shaking him gently, talking to him, until the fog of panic seemed to shred. Haltingly, in broken sentences, Gordon told them what had happened.

As he talked he saw Opal's face appear above him. Vaguely, he wondered how she had gotten back from town so soon, and realized Adam Chaney must have brought her. She had lived here with her aunt and uncle ever since her parents' death. Doorlight made a yellow fire in her hair and she couldn't keep the shock from her face.

Her aunt stood beside her. Charlotte Bayard was a perfumed, bustled, crinolined creature, somewhere far outside Gordon's world. She kept making squeaky sounds, and her soft hands fluttered like birds around her mouth.

"He's bleeding on the porch," she said. "Can't you take him somewhere?"

"Aunt Charlotte," Opal said sharply. It stopped the older woman, and Opal turned to Chaney. "Get him inside. I'll put some water on to boil—there's some arnica—"

She hurried back into the house. Chaney was still crouched beside Gordon, looking up at Bayard. Bayard frowned. Muscle made a spastic little tic in his florid jowl. Then he shook his head and bent to help Chaney lift Gordon onto his feet.

The parlor was all Charlotte Bayard. Its scent of perfume and flowers and incense was so heavy it almost made Gordon sick. The furniture made him think of the stuffed, padded, draped, silken fancy women he had seen promenading down Main. There were lambrequins all over

15

every mantel and lampshade and windowseat. Gordon didn't see how any woman could knot together that much ecru twine in her whole life. Charlotte must have had some time left over, though, because there were about a hundred samplers. WELCOME. GOD BLESS THIS HAPPY HOME. The embroidered mottoes hung on every wall.

Chaney guided Gordon to a chair and Charlotte made a whimpering sound. "Adam—my good chair—"

Adam Chaney gave his sister a look. Gordon didn't know if it was indulgence or disgust. The man took off his red fustian and spread it over the plush chair. He told Gordon to sit down.

Gordon put his head in his hands. He remembered how he'd been unable to feel anything at the dugout. He had thought something was wrong with him. The shock was wearing off now. There was feeling, a sickness, filling his whole body, worse than any ague he had ever known. He wondered how much of it was grief—how much was shame.

"They're dead," he said. "I run out on them. They're both dead. I run out on them . . ."

"You couldn't do anything else," Chaney said. "What good to stay and fight? Getting killed wouldn't bring them back."

Opal came from the kitchen with a bottle of arnica and clean towels. Gordon had ripped his clothes on the bottomland brush and his body was covered with scratches and bruises. Opal began cleaning his wounds and the sting of arnica made him wince. Charlotte had taken a seat on a haircloth settee, as far across the room as she could get. She had a lace handkerchief to her face and was sniffling.

"Roland . . . my camomile pills—this has brought back my vapors."

Her husband didn't seem to hear her. He was pacing back and forth. The room was littered with fat pillows and he had to keep kicking them out of the way. He wheezed faintly as he moved. Roland Bayard must have been a powerful man once, but luxury had turned him heavy and soft. His handsome head was bowed, a mass of ink-black hair fading into distinguished gray sideburns.

"We need protection," Charlotte said, trying again. "Sheriff Simms. Can't you send for Sheriff Simms?"

"Charlotte, Charlotte," Bayard said. He sounded as

16

though he were speaking to a child. "If Simms couldn't stop them in town he certainly couldn't do anything now."

"I can't leave them," Gordon said. "My folks—I got to go back. I got to bury them . . . do something."

"Too dangerous," Chaney said. "The good neighbors of mine—the cattlemen—have had their taste of blood now." He sounded bitter. "A shooting—one of them killed. Your father was a rustler in their eyes, Gordon. Now he's a killer . . . and you're tarred with the same brush. To let one of the big ranchers see you in this basin—it would be worth your life."

"We'll hide him," Bayard said.

"No, no," Charlotte wailed. She half-rose from the settee, her face strained.

"Charlotte's right," Chaney said. "You can't expose her and Opal to the same thing that happened to Conners. If the cattlemen connect you with Conners, find out you're shielding a rustler—"

"That's absurd," Bayard said. "Gordon's got to stay here."

"Got to?" Chaney asked.

Bayard gaped at him. "Well, I— Bob Conners was my friend, I can't let his son—"

"You'd be doing his son a favor to get him out of the country," Chaney said. "I won't let you put my sister in such danger, Roland."

Bayard's face flushed darkly. Gordon couldn't tell whether Chaney was staring at the man, or at some point in the distance. It had a disconcerting effect. Bayard finally shook his head. It made a faint quiver run through his jowls.

"Of course . . . I wasn't thinking. Why don't you go down to the barn and saddle a horse for him, Adam? We'll get some things together here, some decent clothes for him." Chaney nodded and went out. Bayard turned to Opal. "See what food there is. Anything cold—biscuits, some of that roast. There are saddlebags on the back porch."

Opal left immediately and Bayard looked at his wife. "My sack coat and brown pants, upstairs."

Charlotte's stays creaked faintly. "Roland, I—"

"Dear," he said. "Please."

She made a helpless little sound and went upstairs, dabbing at her eyes. Bayard frowned thoughtfully. He and Gordon were alone in the room.

17

"Gordon," Bayard said, "did your father give you anything?"

Gordon looked up numbly. "What?"

"I mean—there must have been a few minutes—when you saw them coming, when Bob knew what might happen. Did he tell you anything?"

"He told me to come to you."

"I don't mean that. Wasn't there something else? Didn't he give you anything?"

Gordon remembered the wallet. "He gave me his money."

"Money?" Bayard's voice was sharp. "I didn't know he had any."

"He must've had something. Maybe, like you say, he figured what was going to happen—"

"And nothing else. He gave you nothing else."

Gordon shook his head. "Mr. Bayard . . . no—nothing else."

Bayard put his hands on the arms of the chair, leaning close to Gordon. He smelled of pomade and tobacco and fine Cordovan leather. His eyes were brilliant and black.

"Gordon, he must have given you—"

Opal came into the room, stuffing a package into a pair of saddlebags. "There wasn't much," she said anxiously. "It might last him a couple of days, if he's careful."

Bayard straightened sharply. He took the saddlebags from her and said, "Go upstairs and stay with your aunt. She's been upset enough for one night."

"Uncle Roland, I—"

"Do as I say, Opal. Tell her I'll come up after the clothes myself."

Opal bit her lip. She glanced at Gordon, then turned and started upstairs. She was halfway up when Gordon heard the sound of horses approaching. A moment later Chaney came in.

"I brought the horse you rode from town," he told Bayard. "You'd left the saddle on. No time to lose, Roland. A lot of riders coming up the creek road."

Charlotte appeared on the landing with the coat and pants. Opal hurried up to take them from her. Bayard studied Gordon, his swarthy cheeks puffed out thoughtfully. Then he slung the saddlebags over Gordon's shoulder. Chaney unstrapped his gunbelt and held the whole harness out to Gordon. The big single-action Colt in the holster had stag grips and its metalwork was tarnished.

18

"No," Gordon said. "I mean, no, I don't want to—"

"Take it," Chaney urged. "You won't stand a chance without one. You'll have to use it to eat on before you're through."

He thrust it into Gordon's hand and turned away toward the door before Gordon could protest. Numbly, recoiling from the sinister weight of the gun hanging against his hands, he buckled the belt on. Opal had hurried downstairs with the clothes and she crossed the room and gave them to Gordon. Her hand remained on his arm. She moistened her lips, and there was something in her eyes.

"Gordon—"

She trailed off. He didn't know what to say. He didn't feel like he was standing up in front of a schoolmarm any longer. He wanted to tell her that, but he thought it would just sound jugheaded. If he could only stay around a while, maybe he could explain it to her. He realized this was probably the last time he would ever see her.

Bayard put a hand on his shoulder. "Gordon, let me know where you are. If you need any more help, money or anything—well, let me know."

"Thanks," Gordon said. "I wish pa knew what good friends you really are."

"Gordon," Chaney called from the door. "Hurry up."

He went outside and saw Chaney holding a horse. Bayard kept the best animals in Table Rock. It was a Morgan, with a coat like satin. Gordon dropped the saddlebags behind the cantle and stepped aboard. The poplar grove still shielded him but he could already feel the ground trembling beneath the approaching riders.

He touched heels to the Morgan and it broke into a nervous canter. The last Gordon saw of Opal she was standing in the open door with the backlight turning her hair to a yellow nimbus.

Chapter Three

THE NUMBNESS BEGAN to creep through Gordon again, as he crossed the basin toward the foothills. He was beaten, exhausted; he seemed incapable of any more strong feeling. The grief and the shame had joined his misery.

He avoided the pass, crossing the ridge far west of town. The smell of sulphur came to him as he topped the caprock. He looked for pursuit in the basin below but could see no sign of it. Either the riders had not guessed he was at the Bayards, or the Bayards had put them off the track. Gordon remembered what his father had said about Blackhorn . . . in the Wind Rivers somewhere, near South Pass City. It seemed a futile destination, hunting for a man he had never seen. But it was all he had left.

The South Pass Mail Road led north out of Table Rock. It took him into the mountains soon, spicy forests of fir, black with lichen on the northern slopes. He dozed in the saddle, he didn't know how often, or how long. He rode till dawn filtered its eery undersea light through the timber and then the sun came up and touched the bright red spikes and orange blossoms on the giant firs and seemed to light their tops afire. Gordon pulled off the road and found a spring in a high park. He watered his horse and ate the cold biscuits and meat Opal had put in the saddlebags. His eyes burned and watered. There was such a powerful ache in his joints he thought he was getting the miseries. The Mail Road was far below him, a yellow thread appearing fitfully in the massed green of the timber.

Gordon saw movement, a rider, ant-size, appearing from the trees, swallowed again in their shadow, moving north along the road. Gordon began to shiver. He led the Morgan into the trees quickly and tightened the latigo. He couldn't stop shaking. He got into the saddle again. He cursed himself. He couldn't honestly say he was afraid. Why was he shaking?

He figured that if the man was following him, and looking for tracks, he would see where Gordon had pulled off the road. Gordon climbed to timberline and over a windswept ridge and found a creek on the other side where he could hide his sign for a space.

As he rode, the gun pressed its weight against his leg. He'd already had the impulse to throw it away, a dozen times over. But he knew Bayard was right. He was going to need it to stay alive. He despised his fear of guns. He didn't know why he feared them. Sometimes he thought it was the sound, actually hurting his ears. Sometimes he thought the pain was only in his mind. His whole life had been haunted by it. When it first appeared his father had tried to punish him out of it. Whenever Gordon shied at gunsound Bob Conners took the horsewhip to him. When that failed he had chained Gordon to a log and shot up a whole box of shells five feet from the boy. It had left Gordon in hysterics. He knew his father was only doing it for his own good. They lived in a land where a man needed a gun to survive. When they had come into the country the Indians were still on the warpath, and the hunt was a daily thing. There had probably never been a day in Bob Conners' life that a gun had not been on him or near at hand. It was unthinkable to him that his son should be so afraid of guns.

Gordon remembered the doctors they had gone to. The one in Laramie had said the boy was of a nervous disposition. That might account for some of it. The one in Cheyenne had tested his reflexes . . . a little hammer tapping his knee and the leg popping up. Unusually quick reflexes, the doctor said. Almost too quick. Some physical source. Definitely some physical source. He prescribed laudanum, to quiet the boy's nerves. A horse doctor at Julesburg had suggested putting cotton in his ears, to muffle the sound, and then shooting a gun off. It hadn't helped. . . .

In the afternoon Gordon cut back over the ridge, found the Mail Road below him again, and watched it from cover till he was sure it was empty. Keeping to high timber, he followed the road on north. It ran through the long trough of South Pass and entered a sagebrush wasteland. Near evening, in this desolation, Gordon found the town.

Gaping adits and rotting flumes and other signs of old diggings were everywhere. Gordon had heard that ten years ago there were four thousand people in South Pass City, but they had abandoned it when the veins pinched out. He entered the ghost town, winding his way through the grass-grown placer ditches and crumbling sluice boxes to one of the rotting cabins. When he pushed on the door it fell in before him, striking the floor with a muffled crash that lifted ancient dust against his face.

He was afraid firelight would give him away. All he had to tether his horse with was the reins. He hitched it outside the cabin and spent a miserable night, hungry, shivering, dreaming.

He dreamed he was locked in a little room again, so

small he couldn't turn around, like a coffin would be, only his father was in it with him, and he couldn't cipher out how the room could be so small and his father so big, towering, a giant, casting his monstrous shadow across Gordon no matter where Gordon turned. His father was shooting off the gun. It crashed and boomed like a mountain falling down, like the world splitting open, and Gordon kept screaming and beating on the walls and all the time the noise kept getting louder, until he knew it was going to bust his head wide open, and his father kept getting bigger, and the room kept getting smaller, till it was so small he couldn't breathe, till the coffin was like an iron band around his chest, squeezing all the air out, suffocating him.

He woke up. He was shaking and making weird sounds in his throat. He was drenched with sweat. He couldn't stand to stay inside the cabin and he crawled on his hands and knees out the door and sprawled weakly on the earth outside. It was an old dream. It always left him drained, spent.

When he recovered he got shakily to his feet. He didn't want to go back inside. He was afraid to sleep again. He went around the shack to check his horse. It was gone. Apparently it had pulled loose while he slept and drifted away. He knew the futility of trying to track it in the dark. He waited till dawn, but he soon lost its sign in the rubble of the town.

Big Hermit Creek ran at the edge of town. He drank and washed in the brackish water, miserably trying to decide what to do. He knew about the only traffic he could count on was the weekly stage from Table Rock to Fort Washakie. They might give him a lift to the nearest way station. The outlying stations had a hard time keeping help and there might be a chance of getting a job wrangling the stage teams until he could get a lead on Blackhorn. The Indians were always drifting past the stations, and his father had said the Indians knew where Blackhorn was. It was a thin hope, but it was all he could think of. He didn't even know what Blackhorn could do when he found the man. About all he expected was some help getting out of the country.

In the meantime he knew he would have to do something about food. The stage might not be along for days. His belly ached and he was already getting dizzy with hunger. Walking back through town he saw gophers tunneling the main street and kept flushing jackrabbits from the weeds.

He stopped in the street. It took a long time before he could make himself pull the gun Chaney had given him. He held the heavy Colt in his hands and stared fixedly at it. It wasn't that he didn't know how to use one. His father had forced him to learn the handling of a gun, both six-shooter and rifle, even though he could never get Gordon to do any shooting. He had to shoot now. He would starve to death if he didn't. He couldn't let his fear kill him.

A cold sweat broke out at his temples. He began to move again. Another jack broke from behind one of the shacks, bounding across Gordon's path. Gordon made a strained sound, lifted the gun. He had the rabbit in front of his sights. When he squeezed the trigger he shut his eyes. The crash of the shot made him shout.

He flung the gun from him. He turned and ran. After the first few steps he stopped himself. He stood shaking, his head bowed, his fists knotted, fighting the panic. He lifted his head and saw the jack far in the distance, bounding away unharmed. He felt a moment of relief. He had never been able to kill anything, or to watch it die. He remembered the first time his father had made him go hunting. Watching the first deer his father shot, watching it squeal and jump and fall, and lie kicking its life out on the ground. It had made him sick.

The rabbit was out of sight. Gordon's relief faded and he couldn't feel anything. He couldn't even feel the usual helpless disgust with himself. It seemed he was too beaten to care any more.

He left the gun where he had thrown it, near the door of the first shack he had slept in. He went back to the creek, hunting berries. He found some chokecherries and ate too many and bloated up like a heifer with colic.

He went back to the shack and lay down, groaning in misery. He was still lying on the floor when he heard the horse whinny from the west end of town. He crawled to the door and looked down the street.

A man came into view. He had his gun out and was leading a horse with a Crazy Moon brand. It was Tom Union.

He was the only cowhand Gordon had ever seen who wore a hard hat. It was round-topped and black and so

23

battered that Gordon thought he must sleep on it. Union was an immensely tall man with an undershot jaw puckered by smallpox scars. His longhorn mustache was stained yellow by chewing tobacco. A chaw always made a leathery bulge in one cheek. He ground on it as placidly as a cow with its cud, his eyes half-closed in bovine contentment, the methodical movement of his jaws making the shiny bulge move up and down his cheek like a loose goiter.

He stopped at each building, searching for fresh sign around the door, and then looking carefully inside. Gordon thought it was mighty careless, until he realized the implications. The man was hunting for Gordon Conners. He must be pretty certain there wouldn't be any shooting.

Gordon crouched in the door, staring hopelessly at the Colt where he had thrown it, only a few feet from the door. He might get it without being seen, but he knew Union was right. He couldn't shoot, even as much as he might secretly wish to. Union had been with the bunch that had killed his parents. Perhaps a bullet from Union's gun had smashed Bob Conners' face. Another bullet could have finished his mother. Tears stung his eyes. He remembered the fiasco with the rabbit. He might tell himself he could shoot, but when it came time, he knew he couldn't.

He wondered why that was all he feared. He realized he didn't feel any particular fear of Union. The man was out to kill him. He represented much more danger than the mere sound of a gun.

Gordon knew it was futile to run. There was too much open country with no cover, once he left town. Union would see him. He would be as helpless as that flushed jack.

He was still staring emptily at the Colt on the ground when it struck him that he might not have to shoot. He might still have a chance.

Union was moving slowly up the street, inspecting each shack. When he found no sign around the door he took the extra precaution of glancing inside. Gordon had left sign all around the building in which he hid. It would give him away before Union got within twenty feet.

But if he could get to one of those other shacks, where there was no sign. A shack Union would reach before this one. If he could find a back way in . . .

He watched until Union reached a turn in the street.

24

For a few minutes the man was hidden behind a line of tarpaper hovels. Gordon moved from the door, scooping up the Colt. Keeping the building between himself and Union, he moved to the rear of the neighboring shack. There was no back door. Furtively, he darted to the next one. Part of the rear wall was caved in. He slipped through the opening, moved across the littered dirt floor. The front door was half-open, sagging on its hinges. He took his place behnd it. He held the gun by its long blue barrel. It was a club now. When Union glanced in the door, for just an instant, he might be close enough. . .

He strained against the wall, listening. His body began to ache with tension. He wondered how he could be so tense and still not be afraid. He knew how slim his chances were. He wasn't afraid. He wished his father could know that somehow.

He heard Union coming. The horse snorted softly. The hoofbeats made a dim sound in the dusty street, stopped for a while, started again. The sound came closer. But it didn't seem to stop any more. It didn't stop at the next door shack. It was coming toward Gordon's shack. It went on by.

Gordon moved to look out through the crack between the wall and the door. He saw Union leading his horse up the middle of the street, toward the shack where Gordon had slept. The man was looking at the ground as he moved. Gordon realized what had happened. Union had picked up Gordon's prints at one of the spots where he had crossed the street this morning, and was following them to the other shack.

Union's back was to Gordon. He was hardly ten feet away. Gordon had a clear shot at him. All he had to do was reverse the gun and fire. It would avenge his parents, it would save his own life.

He continued to hold the gun by its barrel, unable to do it. He closed his eyes, sick with fury at his own impotence.

When he opened his eyes again he saw that Union had turned off the road. The man had seen the tracks of Gordon's horse. He stood near the shack, studying the ground where the Morgan had been hitched. Finally he mounted his horse and headed slowly toward the sagebrush hills. The shiny bulge was sliding methodically up and down his cheek and he was studying the ground as he went, following the trail left by the drifting Morgan.

Gordon leaned against the wall. He felt weak. He felt

foolish. He wondered if he really could have hit Union.

He allowed Union wasn't such a prime tracker after all. It was logical for the man to assume that Gordon had ridden away. But any tracker who really knew his business would realize the prints weren't deep enough for a ridden horse.

Gordon put the gun in its holster. He knew he couldn't stay in South Pass City any longer. Union might find the horse and return. Or there might be other Crazy Moon riders with him. All Gordon could do was head northward. There was bound to be a way station within fifteen or twenty miles.

He moved across a sagebrush land white with salt deposits that had a blinding glare in the sun. The wind blew a chalky sand against him all afternoon till he was powdered from head to foot. On the blinding glare of salt flats he saw a rider. He hid for an hour in the greasewood. When nobody came he thought it must have been a mirage.

The road led him into the Wind Rivers by nightfall. He was stumbling, exhausted, dizzy with hunger. He got the idea again that somebody was following. He stopped and tried to sight them and couldn't. He jumped a foot when an owl hooted at him. It sounded like the wheezing scrape of a distant bucksaw. He moved off the road into the cover of timber. He began to shiver uncontrollably. He had heard of the glaciers up here that never melted. He could see them through the timber, high above, where nothing grew, white and shimmering under a rising moon. Finally he could go no farther and he sank down against an aspen. He felt drugged. He must have slept. Then he was being shaken. Somebody's hand on his shoulder, shaking him awake. He opened his eyes to see a seamed, bearded face. Beyond the face was a horse. There was a Crazy Moon brand on its hip.

"Git up, sonny," the man said. "I been afollerin' you a long time."

There seemed to be a weight against Gordon's chest, a suffocating weight. His legs had gone to sleep, doubled under him, and he could hardly stand up. He held himself rigidly against the tree, speaking thickly.

"Which one are you?" he asked. "I never seen you with MacLane before."

"I'm Blackhorn," the man said.

Chapter Four

THERE WAS A SPARE horse for Gordon, another Crazy
Moon animal with a rawhide-laced saddle. They rode into
the deep blackness of the timber and Blackhorn was only
a shadow behind him. Gordon started to speak again but
Blackhorn told him to shut up. Fear kept him alert for
awhile but then the starved dizziness came back and he
began to sway in the saddle. He must have passed out. He
came to once, tied on the horse. Then the blackness closed
in again. He couldn't fight any longer. He didn't seem to
care any more . . .

When he regained consciousness he was lying beneath
a buffalo robe, musky with age and riddled with bot holes.
Firelight played uncertainly across a calico mule and
three horses hitched to a line between two trees. Camp
gear was strewn across the ground—blanket rolls, more
buffalo robes, an army pack saddle, tinware, a rifle in a
fringed saddle boot. The fire was built in a circle of stones.
Beside it crouched the man, watching Gordon.

It was the same pleated face, half-hidden in a curly red
beard, ruddy as the flames. The squinted eyes were almost lost in the network of wrinkles surrounding them.
The nose was hooked and had been broken and knocked
over to one side by some former blow. The hands, resting
on the man's legs, were as seamed from weather and use
as his face, covered with fresh scars that looked like rope
burns, and older scars that looked like something else.
He was dressed in the filthiest rawhide shirt and leggings
Gordon had ever seen, with a pair of black-butted Navy
Colts in homemade horsehide holsters, hitched around to
lay in his lap with the ends pointed inward. He chuckled,
finally, and it revealed his yellow teeth.

"Booger," he said. "You can talk now. Ain't no MacLane
men around to hear."

Gordon shook his head, trying to get the clabber out
of his brains. "You ain't with MacLane?" he asked.

"Why should I be?"

"Those horses—I saw the Crazy Moon . . ."

Blackhorn slapped his leg, laughing uproariously. "By
gannies, you did, at that. Some Crazy Moon riders was

camped along the South Pass Mail Road, about a day north of Table Rock. A couple of 'em are agoin' to have a powerful long walk back to town."

"MacLane will string you up."

The man grinned roguishly. "If every man that I stole a horse from was to string me up, they'd need more rope than there is hemp."

Gordon sank weakly against the bunk. "You said you'd been followin' me a long time."

"I judged you'd be comin' up my way," Blackhorn said. "I kept in touch with your pa. I used to see him once in a while, out on the range. He asked me once, if he got in a fix, could he send you and Sarah along to old Blackhorn for safe keeping. He knew I was somewhere around South Pass City. When I heard MacLane had killed your folks—"

"How did you hear about that?"

"The leaves rustle, sonny. The Injuns talk. They know what goes on in a country, faster than any white man. I kept my eyes peeled. I saw the MacLane riders and guessed what was up. I cut your sign near South Pass City and follered you out from there. Life ain't really so complicated, is it?"

Gordon gazed at the satanic old face, trying to decide whether he felt safe at last or not. The sly twinkle in the man's faded blue eyes disturbed him. Blackhorn looked aside sharply. A girl entered camp carrying a bullhide pail of water. At first Gordon thought she was Indian. She carried the pail to the fire, set it down, and stood silently regarding Gordon. He felt embarrassed, being caught in bed by a girl. He threw the robe off and sat up. Blackhorn chuckled slyly.

"This is Willa, my daughter. Her ma was a Dakota."

She was cleaner than most half-breeds Gordon had seen. Her buckskin dress was white, paper-thin and satiny from a hundred washings on river stones. Her hair didn't have the dead, horse-mane coarseness he was used to in the Indians. The highlights seemed to glow with a rusty fire and the hair fell in loose, natural curls that must have come from Blackhorn. Her eyes were onyx, staring at him solemnly. But there was a dimple in one cheek, the hint of a smile that made him think of the rollicking Indian babies he had seen at Table Rock. He had always wondered why the Indians stopped laughing in front of white men, when they grew up.

Blackhorn made a snarling sound. "Don't stand there agapin'," he told the girl. "Git the boy somethin' to eat. Never git mixed up with a squaw, Gordon. Lazy, dirty, lyin'—you can't do nothin' with 'em but cut off their hair and flog 'em every day."

The girl's hand went automatically to her hair. He picked up one of the rocks circling the fire and threw it. She danced to avoid it. Her eyes downcast, she wheeled quickly and dipped up some soup that had been simmering in a pot hung on a gaunch hook over the flames. She brought it to Gordon in a wooden bowl, along with a slab of pemmican.

"Now," Blackhorn said, "go and rub down them animals. If I find any gall sores on your pony you'll go without eatin' tomorrow."

Gordon watched the girl move toward the horses. She didn't seem frightened or resentful. She had the stoic, withdrawn look he had seen in so many squaws along the tracks. While Gordon ate, the old man dipped himself out some soup. He gulped it noisily, spilling it into his beard and on his shirt. When he was through he belched.

"Miserable cooks, too," he said. "Worst cooks in the world. So MacLane's on your tail?"

Gordon was still eating. "He thought pa rustled his stock. There was a fight . . . pa killed one of MacLane's hands."

"Well, I suppose that does have some bearing. But we know what's really on MacLane's mind."

"Pa didn't rustle those cattle."

"Of course he didn't. MacLane just needed an excuse. I wouldn't doubt but what MacLane had somebody plant that beef there himself. He had to git rid of your pa somewhere."

"*Had* to?"

Blackhorn looked up at him coldly. "Sonny . . . you know what I'm talking about."

"No I don't."

"You mean you don't know why MacLane's really after you? Your pa never told you?"

"Told me what?"

Blackhorn made a soft whistling sound. "Well, now. If that ain't hark from the tomb." He grimaced and scratched his ear. "Howsomeever, I guess I can understand. Your pa, he wasn't a natural-born thief like me. He went into it because he was desperate. I guess he was

29

powerful ashamed. I guess that's why he never told you."

"Blackhorn, will you quit—"

Blackhorn held up a scarred hand, cutting Gordon off. The old man seated himself on a robe, and dropped his hand back in his lap, looking beyond Gordon.

"It happened twenty years ago," Blackhorn said. "Just a couple of months after you come along. Gittin' you foaled had caused your ma a heap of trouble and they thought she was agoin' to die. The doctor at Cheyenne said the only thing that could save her was some hospital, in the East. It was agoin' to take a lot of money, and your pa was dead broke. This was in '65, mind you, when the railroad was abuildin' west. Your pa and me was hunting buffalo at the time, supplying the tracklayers with meat. One of the other hunters was named Tom Union—"

"Tom Union!"

"Don't interrupt, dammit. This Tom Union knew what a spot your pa was in, told us he had a way we could git the money. Your pa was willing to do anything. It had to do with the pay train. I don't know how many thousand men was abuildin' that track, but you can imagine what a payroll the Union Pacific had each month. The jasper planning this robbery was with the railroad. He could git us Pinkerton credentials and git us aboard the pay car as guards."

"Who was he?"

"I never saw him, and Tom Union never said who he was. The only contact Union claimed to have with him was by mail. When Tom Union give us our fake Pinkerton papers, there was a note along with them. It was in a right peculiar style of handwriting. Your pa kept it."

Gordon remembered the wallet his father had given him in the dugout. He had thought it contained money, had told Bayard so. He took it from the inside pocket of the sack coat Bayard had given him. The leather was stiff with dried blood and when he opened the wallet there was no money, only a single, tattered, folded sheet of paper. He opened it. There was a faded note.

The pay train reaches Julesburg on 5:15 on the 9th inst. You will board the red, converted coach and present your Pinkerton credentials to the paymaster. At 10:30 p.m. you will approach Hairpin Crossing. There will be four guards and the paymaster in your car. Once they are under control you will have three minutes on the bridge. You will get five strongboxes and dump them off as the train slows for the curve just beyond the bridge. You will be able to jump off after them. Union and I will be waiting with horses beneath the bridge.

Blackhorn had gotten to his feet, crossing to Gordon and looking at the note. "That's it," he said. "It tells you exactly what happened, except for the end. Everything went slick as bear grease. The guards wasn't hard to surprise—them thinkin' we were some o' their own. We dumped the boxes and jumped off. Time we got back to the bridge nobody was there. They musta had pack saddles rigged for those strongboxes. They hadn't even left us no horses. By that time the paymaster had stopped the train, and about fifty men was jumping off after us. With horses we could've got away. Afoot all we could do was hole up under the bridge and fight. It took fifteen or twenty minutes of shootin' before we finally seen it was hopeless and give up. That give Tom Union and his pard just about enough time for a clean getaway. Time that train crew found out we didn't have the money, it was too late. Afterwards, we figured out that's just what Tom Union and Company wanted. Somebody to be the goats. Somebody to keep the train crew pinned down long enough for Union and the other one to make a getaway."

"But ma—you said she was dyin'."

"She come mighty close to it. I guess she would have if the Bayards hadn't took her in—"

"Bayards!"

"That's right. Roland Bayard was a dispatcher for the railroad at the time, working out of Julesburg. You and your ma lived with 'em, while me and your pa was in jail. You put some animals in a cage and they die, sonny. That's what was happenin' to me. I knew I couldn't last for ten years. About the second year, your pa and me escaped . . ."

Gordon looked unseeingly at the note. So many things made sense now. So many strange quirks that had puzzled him in his father. How they were always on the move, never settling long in one spot. How Bob Conners had always made sure there was a back door out of his place, even a dugout. The ways of a wanted man. But had it been his fear of the law—or of something else?

31

"You said MacLane had to git rid of pa," Gordon said. "Do you think MacLane was the man who planned that robbery?"

"Don't it add up? You said your pa didn't rustle the cattle. And Tom Union is MacLane's man again, ain't he? Jist like in the holdup. You ever seen MacLane's handwriting?"

"No," Gordon said.

"That was MacLane's mistake, writing that note. Match the note with his handwriting and you got the proof that would involve him in the robbery. Your pa had evidence that would ruin MacLane, would send him to prison for ten years. When your pa showed up in Table Rock, MacLane knew he couldn't be there for anything besides revenge."

"Why didn't MacLane just have him shot?"

"Maybe he tried that too."

"I guess he did," Gordon said softly. He was remembering the night two months ago when his father had come home during a rainstorm. He was afoot, and said he'd lost his horse. There was a tear in his slicker, and a haunted look in his face. Gordon looked again at the paper in his hand.

"That's right," Blackhorn said. "And now you got the note." Gordon raised his eyes slowly. Blackhorn made a snorting sound. "Don't look at me. I don't want it. Them other Crazy Moon hands might've been trailin' you because your pa killed one of 'em. Union was after you for that note. A smart fox knows when to run, jigger. Your pa ain't alive, and I am. I'm too old for revenge. I'll git you outa this country but then you're on your own. I'm even ashamed of myself for doin' that much. It ain't becomin' to the greatest horse thief in the world."

The food made Gordon drowsy. He tried to stay awake, to think. What Blackhorn said made sense. But he still couldn't find his place in it. He couldn't see any daylight. Did it mean he had to run for the rest of his life, the way his father had been running?

He finally dozed off. When he woke again he saw that the fire had died down. It made a dim red glow against Willa, sleeping under a buffalo robe. Blackhorn sat upright against a tree, snoring softly.

Gordon started to lift his cover off and swing his legs out. There was no obvious change from sleeping to waking in Blackhorn. He merely came up on his feet and pulled his guns out.

"Somebody around?" Blackhorn said.

"No," Gordon said. "I guess it was me."

"Booger! Be a mite more careful. I mighta shot you."
He peered at Gordon. "I guess I ain't the only one's
jumpy."

Gordon realized how he had jumped back, all tangled
up with the robe. His attention was riveted on the guns.
Blackhorn put them away. He squinted at Gordon,
scratching his beard.

"I had a dog that was gun shy once," he said. "I always
figured it went back to the time he was a pup and some
kids shot a gun off a couple dozen times, just to see him
jump and howl."

"Pa used to do that. He said it would cure me. When I
was about four he locked the two of us in a room and shot
his gun off out the window for about an hour."

"Hark from the tomb. If you wasn't gun shy before,
that'd sure do the job." Blackhorn picked a black louse
from his beard, studied it thoughtfully, and squashed it
between his thumb and forefinger. "Well, your pa never
did have a lot of imagination. Suppose your life depended
on it. Suppose you was starving, and you had a gun, and a
deer was standing smack dab in front of you."

"It was. I mean—the rabbit . . . Adam Chaney gave me
a gun. I tried to shoot. Every time—I closed my eyes. I
can't stand to see the animal hit. Dad took me hunting a
dozen times. It was never any good."

Blackhorn was studying him. "Maybe your own life ain't
enough. Maybe it's got to be somethin' else."

"I don't follow you."

"Well, you take an animal now. It's the taste of blood
that drives them wild, ain't it? You can turn a tame dog
into a killer . . ."

Willa made a soft sound. It made Gordon look at her.
He wondered how long she had been lying there, awake,
staring at him.

Chapter Five

THE NEXT MORNING after breakfast Blackhorn saddled his
calico mule. He slung his rifle in its fringed saddleboot
under one stirrup leather. He said he was going to scout

33

their backtrail for signs of the Crazy Moon men.

"When you finish makin' that pemmican," he told Willa, "you kin pick up camp. I want everything packed and ready to go when I git back."

She watched him as he rode off. Her eyes were heavy-lidded, smoky, unreadable.

"He works you like a dog," Gordon said.

"Like a squaw," she said.

"Why don't you leave him?"

"He is my father," she said.

She crossed to a purple heap of chokecherries that she had apparently gathered the day before. She knelt and began pulverizing them a handful at a time in a wooden bowl. He watched idly, wondering why he didn't feel uncomfortable with her, the way he had with Opal, with so many other girls. There was something shy about her, submissive, completely accepting. But there was something strong about her too, a core that Blackhorn's treatment could never touch. She didn't tease or joke or play coy little games. She wouldn't get all fussed up if a man cussed or happened to belch. Gordon's clothes were filthy, his face still caked with alkali dust, his shirt torn and his shaggy black hair matted with burrs. Opal would've been letting him know how she felt about that every time she looked at him. For all Willa let on, he might have been dressed in the most elegant suit in Omaha. He crossed and knelt beside her.

"I'll help."

She let him mash the berries while she got some strips of dried meat and pounded it into a powder with a stone maul. It had always been hard for him to carry on a conversation with a girl.

"Blackhorn said your ma was Indian," he said.

"She was a Dakota. She died when I was a little girl."

"And you been living with Blackhorn ever since. All this talk he makes—him bein' the greatest horse thief in the world, is that really true?"

"Among my mother's people it is counted a great coup for a boy to steal the horse of an enemy," she said. "When the berries are all paste, let them dry in the sun."

When the paste was partially dry she mixed it with the ground meat and some melted fat, forming it all into a cake. She set the cake out to dry. On her knees, making another cake, she spoke again.

"I do not like guns either. The sound of them either. The sound of them makes me afraid too."

He looked down at his hands. He didn't want to talk about it. The people of his world hadn't understood it. He didn't understand it himself. How could he explain it to Willa?

"My mother used to tell me stories," Willa said. "One of them was about her father, who was Fox Dreamer. When he was a young man Fox Dreamer would not go on the buffalo hunt. His people said he was afraid of the buffalo and called him an ugly name. One time a child fell into the river. It was in flood. It was full of ice. The people said anybody would be killed if they went into it. They would not stay alive. None of the braves would go into it. Fox Dreamer went into it and saved the child. After that the people forgot the ugly names. My mother said there are many ways of being brave."

Gordon frowned at her. He sensed something behind the story. Was it her way of showing sympathy? He was surprised that he felt none of the shame he had known with his father or Opal when his fear of guns had come up.

He heard a faint stir at the edge of the clearing and turned to see Blackhorn sitting his mule there. The old man was scowling at them, fraying his beard with knobby fingers.

"That's a right smart story," he told Willa. "You never told me that story before."

Willa looked at him, then quickly at the ground. "My mother told me the story."

"Fox Dreamer. Was that your grandpa's name? When I give him twenty horses for your mother his name was Great Cloud."

"Fox Dreamer was also his name."

The girl's face was turned down but Gordon thought he saw a faint flush in her cheek. Blackhorn swung out of the saddle, looking around camp.

"I told you to have things packed," he said to Willa. He walked toward her, bowlegged, shuffle-footed, rolling from side to side like a tipsy bear. "Lyin' around camp, fat and sassy, spinnin' yarns, tellin' lies, wastin' time, while I was out workin' my tail off, riskin' my scalp to make things snug and tight for you. It's about time you had a lesson." He pulled his knife as he reached her. He grabbed her by the hair, lifting her to her feet. "I'm agoin' to

35

shave off your pelt. I'm agoin' to leave you skinned and pink as a new baby—"

"No!" She caught at her hair, trying to pull away. Her face was white, contorted. "No, Blackhorn, please—"

Maybe it was the look in her face. Gordon did it without thinking. He jumped up and lunged at Blackhorn, grabbing his wrist. He twisted it back till Blackhorn howled and dropped the knife. Blackhorn let go of Willa with his other hand and pulled one of his Navy Colts. Gordon thought he was going to shoot and released his wrist.

Gordon pushed the girl behind him. "Leave her alone," he warned Blackhorn.

Blackhorn regarded him a moment, then said with an ugly note in his voice, "Afraid to shoot off a gun. But you talk big when you're not wearin' one."

"You got no right to cut off her hair."

Blackhorn rubbed a hand across his mouth, then holstered his Colt. Gordon breathed easier. He had not known until that minute whether the old man would shoot him or not. Behind him Willa made a soft sound.

"I never cut Willa's hair off," Blackhorn said, "and she knows it. If a body don't put a little green fear in these squaws once in a while they'll git as uppity as any St. Looey fancy woman. Start breakin' camp, Willa. I've had my craw full of your fooforaw."

The girl started gathering the robes. Blackhorn shouldered the blanket roll and crossed to lash it behind the saddle of his calico mule. Gordon allowed the mule must be about as ornery as Blackhorn. Every time Blackhorn turned his back it nipped at him. Gordon understood why there were so many patches on his britches.

With Blackhorn on the mule, and the two stolen horses carrying the camp gear, there was only one horse left to ride. Blackhorn told Gordon to get on. He thought Willa would mount behind him. Blackhorn shouted and whacked the horses and got them underway. Gordon looked back to see Willa following afoot. He tried to rein in. Blackhorn pulled the reins from his hands and rode ahead, leading Gordon's horse into a canter.

"Leave her be," Blackhorn said. "She's got to have some kind of lesson. She won't waste so much time around the next camp."

"It ain't right," Gordon said.

"She's my daughter." Blackhorn glared back at him. "You butted in once today and you still got a whole skull.

Don't press your luck, sonny."

They moved northward into the Wind Rivers. It was a wilderness of vast silences, mist-hung valleys, black-shadowed timber. Glaciers that never melted glistened on the peaks above, and the wind roared through thick stands of pine like some distant surf. They struck a dim game trail and followed it through timber so lush it was almost tropical. Yellow autumn ferns rustled beneath tall firs and the leaves of ash made a silver shimmer in the glens.

Gordon looked back at Willa. Blackhorn was moving the horses along at a pace faster than an ordinary walk and Willa was having a hard time keeping up.

Half the time she had to trot. She was winded, her face grimed with sweat, for this had been going on most of the morning. The trail was rough and steep, and she kept stumbling. He saw that her moccasins had been torn somewhere on the rocks. Some of her prints were darkened by a stain of blood. She began losing ground, dropping back. In running to catch up, she stumbled and fell.

Gordon dropped off his horse. He ran forward to grab the reins near the bit, jerking them from Blackhorn's hand. Blackhorn turned savagely toward him.

"Git back on that horse."

"She's going to ride," Gordon said.

"She's my daughter. I got the say of whether she walks or rides!"

"Not now, old man," Gordon said.

A grimace of rage deepened the pleats in Blackhorn's face. For a moment Gordon thought the old man was going to pull his gun. Then he thought Blackhorn was going to swing out of the saddle. Gordon waited, staring doggedly at him. When Blackhorn didn't do anything, Gordon led the horse back to Willa. She had regained her feet. She looked solemnly at Gordon, took the reins from his hand, and mounted. Gordon swung up behind the saddle.

Blackhorn was still waiting fifteen feet up the trail, glaring at them. As they started toward him he let out an obscene curse and whacked his mule so hard it squealed and bolted down the trail, the pack horses stampeding ahead of it. Gordon felt Willa's body tremble. He thought she was crying at first. Then he realized it was a giggle.

Blackhorn didn't speak to them for the rest of that day. He rode ahead, studying the ground constantly. The only sign Gordon could see were animal tracks once in a while.

He knew a marten's prints, the paws in pairs, each pair oblique to the other. Farther on something like dog tracks, too broad a straddle for a wolf, probably a wolverine. But no man sign.

They didn't make camp till dusk, halting in a high park near a creek. Gordon dismounted first and helped Willa down. She almost went to her knees and he saw her face draw up in pain. Blackhorn was watching her. As she limped across to one of the packhorses, the old man called sharply to her.

"Willa!"

She turned, surprised. Blackhorn was off his mule. He crossed to the packhorse, pulled out a diamond hitch, and threw one of the loosened buffalo robes on the ground.

"Sit down," he commanded.

Wonderingly, she sat on the robe. The old man jerked the bullhide bucket out of the gear and tossed it to Gordon. Catching it, Gordon glanced at the girl, then went to get water from the creek. Blackhorn had a fire going by the time Gordon returned. He was heating some lard in the frying pan. He told Gordon to get the horn of gunpowder he kept in his gear for reloading. He poured some of the powder into the melted lard, mixed it together with a stick, and carried the sizzling pan over to Willa. He knelt before her and took off her moccasins. His gentleness surprised Gordon. Blackhorn dipped his neckerchief in the pail first, and washed her cut and swollen feet. Then he began to rub them with the hot mixture of lard and gunpowder.

"Old mountain man remedy," he said. "Cures everything from gunshot wound to green sickness."

He cut a strip from the end of a blanket and carefully bandaged her feet. When he was finished she tried to get up. He told her to lie down again, he would fix the vittles. He showed Gordon what a tinipsila root looked like and told him to gather them from around the edges of the park. He shucked them down to the white, turnip-like meat and threw them into the pot with a cake of pemmican for stew. He squatted over the fire, filling the coffee pot. He kept muttering under his breath and it wasn't clear whether he was talking to Gordon or himself.

"I'm an ornery old cuss, jigger. What makes me such an ornery old cuss?"

Gordon glanced at Willa, lying drowsily on the robe, her

face glowing in the warmth of the fire. It didn't seem to make sense. Gordon remembered the same contradiction in his father—the work he had done, the punishment he had taken, the sacrifices he had made to support his family . . . and the times he would whip Gordon bloody for nothing or go for a week without talking to his wife. Maybe something happened to a man who had run for nineteen years. Gordon wondered what would happen to him under that kind of pressure.

After eating, Blackhorn cleaned up, and they turned in. When Gordon woke next morning Willa was already up, heating water over the fire, and Blackhorn was standing at the edge of the park, studying something on the aspens. They were tall trees, slim, pale and smooth as flesh. Gordon saw the slashes on the chalky bark a foot above Blackhorn's head. Blackhorn was running his fingers over the marks.

"Them corky black ones are old scars, these lower down are still wet to the sapwood. Chances are we jist missed runnin' into him last night. Not a brown bear, either. When they're that high it's more likely a grizzly."

"Pa said they did that to sharpen their claws," Gordon said.

"Hogwash. They do it for a brag. A new bear comes into the district, the first thing he does is check the claw marks. If they're taller than his he ain't agoin' to claim the favorite bee tree or the local she-bear, you can wager." He moved around the park, studying the other trees. "The way this place is marked up, it must be a regular meeting house. If there's an onion patch hereabouts we might even fetch ourselves some bear steaks."

He crossed to the gear and pulled out his Joslyn-Tomes, loading it. He looked from Willa to Gordon, a sly twinkle in his eyes. An expression Gordon had seen before. It gave him the look of some devilment on his mind, but Gordon could never be sure. Blackhorn laid the gun across his saddle and walked back to the trees, studying for tracks. He seemed to find some that satisfied him.

"Give me half an hour before breakfast," he said. "They're usually rooting for onions in the morning. If I don't find a patch this side of the ridge I'll come back."

He stalked off into the timber. Gordon looked at Willa. She must have sensed his confusion about Blackhorn.

"Do you know about the buffalo?" she asked. "Have

39

you ever seen a rogue bull?"

"You mean the kind that gets kicked out of the herd?"

"Yes. That kind. Sometimes it happens when they are bad. Sometimes it happens when they are old. They are mean and dangerous. They are unhappy and they don't know why. It must be because they are lonely."

"Yeah," he said. "I reckon as how." He pulled at his jaw. "I should think you'd get lonely too."

"Sometimes."

"You ain't never had . . . what I mean . . . boys . . . you ain't never known any, well, close-like—"

She would not look at him. Her face was turned down and the firelight gave it a coppery glow. She looked so demure, so virginal.

"Blackhorn says I am too young," she said. "But I have seventeen summers. Sometimes I dream. I dream that a young man will come on a spotted pony. The Indians sing songs, you know. They sing songs when they go to war, or when they go on a hunt."

"And this young man, he'll be singing a song?"

"Yes."

"A love song?"

He was surprised at himself after he'd said it. It wasn't the kind of thing he could say so easily, before. He remembered how ashamed he'd felt with Opal. Willa had not looked up. Her lips glistened, full and vividly red.

"Willa," he said softly.

"It is just what Blackhorn calls me," she said. "It is really Wiwilla. In Dakota, it means Spirit of Spring."

"That's nice," he said. "I mean it sounds nice." His palms felt damp. He wiped them against his britches. "This young man— Will he have to come on a spotted pony?"

She raised her head. For an instant the shyness was gone from her eyes. The dimple deepened in one cheek and he thought she was going to smile. Before he could tell the water began to boil and she had to run away and move the pot off the flames. It took Gordon's attention off her for the first time since Blackhorn had left, and he noticed the Joslyn-Tomes lying across the saddle.

"He forgot his rifle," he said.

She looked at the gun. "Maybe you'd better take it to him."

He started toward the rifle, then stopped. She looked at

40

him. He felt the deep flush climb into his face. Before he could move again there was a shot up toward the ridge. It echoed down the long aisles of timber, a hollow, shattering sound.

Willa rose to her feet, looking off. "That's close."

Gordon hardly heard. Another shot came, closer, and a third. Something dry and cottony swelled in Gordon's throat. He waited for the echoes to die. They would not die. They seemed to grow louder, multiplying in the timber, making thunderclaps against the sounding boards of the mountains. He didn't know what to do. He started toward the gun. He stopped. He started in another direction and saw Willa looking at him. He stopped again. There would be more shots. He knew there would be more shots.

He heard the sound of running feet and Blackhorn plunged into the clearing, shouting, "Git me my rifle, Gordon. It's Old Ephriam and my smoke pole's jammed. I got one shot in him and he's mad as hell!"

The enraged bear appeared in the timber behind Blackhorn. It was a shadowy figure at first, huge, golden, coming in a lumbering run, the tawny hair of its broad chest curly and matted with blood. Blackhorn was only a few steps into the clearing when he tripped and sprawled onto his face. The bear burst from the trees on his trail, clawing up needles in a glittering shower.

Willa made a broken sound, seized a blazing brand from the fire, and ran at the bear. She reached Blackhorn first, throwing the stick at the oncoming bear. The beast roared and veered away from the hated fire. But it didn't stop.

Willa bent to grab her father, trying to lift him to his feet. Gordon didn't know how the rifle got into his hands. The stock was against his cheek and he was swinging the gun around till the matted, bloody chest covered his sights. He squeezed the trigger. The gun kicked so hard he had to take a step backward.

But his eyes were still open and he saw the impact of the fifty-seventy jar the bear heavily. It made a coughing sound, stumbled on two more steps, and then rolled head over heels and came to a stop with one paw only a few inches from Willa's foot. Willa had stopped trying to get Blackhorn up. She stared down at the shining, curved claws in fascinated horror.

Gordon was staring too. Dazedly. At the claws, at the lathered mouth, gaping open to reveal the ravenous yellow teeth. There was a hot stench to the grizzly even in death. It reached Gordon, heavy with the smell of blood. He thought he was going to be sick. Blackhorn sat up, looking at the bear. He shook his head dazedly.

"Well, appears you saved my hide." He glanced up at the girl, the sly twinkle in his eyes. "Willa's too."

Something about the man's expression disturbed Gordon. It made him remember how Blackhorn had looked when he first found the claw marks. He forced himself to look at the bear. He couldn't understand what was happening to him. He tried to find the revulsion he had felt watching his father shoot a deer or a jack, watching it leap up, fall to the ground, kicking, whimpering.

It wouldn't come. He was merely looking at something that had been moving a moment before, and was not moving now. In a way there was a let-down to it. He almost felt disappointed.

"You done a good job for a boy afraid of guns," Blackhorn said.

"I didn't have time to think," Gordon said. "I don't even remember picking it up."

Blackhorn was on his feet, dusting himself off. "That's what I figured. Right close shave, wasn't it?"

A suspicion was growing in Gordon. "Was it?" he asked.

"Booger! Another six inches and Willa would've been bear-bait."

"Where do you shoot a bear so's you don't kill him—just make him mad enough to chase you?"

"Nothin' madder than a wounded bear," Blackhorn said.

"I guess you know all about bears. I guess you know all about Willa, too. I guess you figgered just about what she'd do."

Blackhorn grinned admiringly at his daughter. "She's a good girl. I treat her ornery as hell sometimes, but she knows I love her."

"Love. What kind of love is that? You must be crazy, she could've been killed—"

Blackhorn looked down at his second Navy revolver, still in its holster. His eyes were squinted almost shut. "Could she?"

42

Gordon didn't think he'd ever been so mad. "You didn't have no right—taking such a chance with her—"

"Chance! What chance? What're you gabblin' about? Everybody fergits somethin' once in a while. The girl wasn't in no danger. You was here, wasn't you?"

"But how could you know, how could you know—?"

"Know what? It was lucky I forgot the gun. You handled it like a veteran. Maybe you learned your lesson. Think you'll ever be afraid of guns again?"

"Just because it happened once—"

"You did it once, you can do it again. You found out it ain't what you thought—shooting something. You found out you could do it when you had to. Maybe an old man in trouble couldn't of made you do it. But a girl—a young buck'll do anything for a pretty girl, won't he?"

Gordon looked at Blackhorn for a long moment. He stared down at the weapon he still held. The weapon, warm from exploding power. Metal, hard in his hands. Lethal. Maybe, he thought, looking at Blackhorn again. Just maybe there had been something to what Blackhorn said.

Chapter Six

THEY MOVED NORTHWARD through the Wind Rivers for two more days. Blackhorn was unusually solicitous with Willa. He even let her ride behind him on his mule sometimes, and the second morning he let her sleep while he gathered water and firewood.

Gordon realized he would never know whether the old man had deliberately created the situation with the bear, or whether it had truly been accidental. He couldn't quite believe that Blackhorn would be callous enough to risk his daughter's life in such a plan. But Blackhorn's own life had been risked too. And if he had done it deliberately, it had been to help Gordon. Gordon couldn't add it up.

Blackhorn told him they were heading for Fort Washakie, where he would try to get a job for Gordon on one of the wagon trains heading east. Gordon started to say he wasn't at all sure he wanted to go East; that he had been doing a lot of thinking these past days. That it had all been crystalized when he saw the dead bear at his feet. And knew he had killed it. But he did not speak. And he was glad. For one side of him still heard the thunder of gunfire and the raw fear climbed swiftly. The other side, the maturing, rational side, was speaking with such a faint voice as to be almost unnoticed.

On the third day they came down out of the Wind Rivers into the endless sage flats. The sage was everywhere, feathery, gray-green, until a body got to thinking it was the only bush in the world. The earth was sandy clay, changing colors as they rode, bone-white along the creek banks, red as blood where there was iron in the ground. It hadn't rained in too long and the wind kept dust devils dancing on the skyline all day long.

They were on the Shoshone reservation. They found a main road and passed wagonloads of Indians all heading in the same direction. Blackhorn said they were going to the fort for their September beef issue. It was a trip that had replaced the fall hunt. Where the Little Wind River met the North Fork they saw Fort Washakie. The log buildings seemed to rise over the horizon like a buffalo herd on the move. There were a dozen buildings, the logs black with age, the adobe water-streaked and crumbling. The Indians were camped in the willow grove around the fort or out on the sage flats. Some of them had buffalohide lodges and some had patched Sibley tents that must have been discarded by the army. Their linchpin wagons were tied together with rope or rawhide; the horses were crowbait; half the women seemed blind or pitted with pox, and the men spent most of their time shivering dismally around the campfires. Gordon didn't think he'd ever seen such a mangy bunch of Indians.

"It's what happens when you tame an Injun," Blackhorn said disgustedly. "Build 'em wood floors and they git consumption. Feed 'em white man's food and their teeth fall out. When I first seen 'em twenty years ago they was the proudest people in God's big pasture."

They stopped before a scabby log building with a sod roof. There was a long cottonwood rack with half a dozen army horses hitched to it and a few bareback Indian ponies. Blackhorn said they would leave their horses and go inside. He wanted to see the sutler about the wagon train and it was necessary to go through the saloon to get to the sutler's store behind.

44

The ceiling inside was so low a tall man would bump his head and smoke from the camphene lamps on the tables made an oily yellow haze. There was sawdust on the clay floor, black with trampling and stinking of spilled whiskey. The bar was no more than a pair of puncheon planks held up at their ends by two barrels. Behind it stood the barkeep, bald and smiling as Buddha, a rusty tin dipper in one hand and a loaded pool cue in the other. Across the front of his padded waistcoat hung an enormous gold chain with an American Horologe watch dangling at one end, and a watchkey shaped like a naked woman hanging at the other.

"It's a bit house," Blackhorn told Gordon. "Horace there will give you a dipper of rotgut from the barrel for one bit, pour it from the bottle for two bits, or draw a charcoal line on the bottle and let you pour your own for four bits. It's pure forty rod. Drop a man to his knees exactly forty rods from where he took his drink. You and Willa stand here in the corner while I find the sutler. Just keep quiet and you won't be troubled. I don't want to go draggin' a filly through all them drunk soldiers."

Blackhorn pushed into the crowd and Gordon saw him disappear through a door that led to another part of the building.

There were some buckskinned trappers in the crowd and a handful of Swede farmers drinking solemnly at one of the deal tables. Most of the customers seemed to be soldiers from the fort. There was a big blond trooper at the bar making a lot of noise. He had a black Jeff Davis hat with the brim looped up on the right side and the crossed sabers of the cavalry pinned to its front. He wore his buff coat belt to hold up his trousers, in defiance of regulations, and his empty saber slings dangled against his leg. He must have been busted to ranks recently because there was a light patch on his sleeve where his stripes had been. When he reached for one of the marked bottles on the bar, Horace rapped him across the knuckles with the loaded cue.

"No more credit on the four-bit drinks, Conway," the barkeep said.

Conway cursed him and lurched away from the bar. He shambled through the crowd, the brass hardware on his saber slings clanking. He tried to borrow from several soldiers, but they all turned him down. By the time he neared Gordon his face was flushed with a sullen anger. He was only a few feet away when his foggy gaze swung across Willa. He stopped, blinking his eyes. He leered drunkenly.

"Y're a new one," he said. "Tell y'r pa I'll give him a jug of whiskey."

Her eyes smoldered. "My father is Blackhorn."

"Talks like a human bein', too," Conway said. He moved toward her, heavy on his feet, and grabbed her arm. "C'mon. Where's your teepee? I'll pay y'r pa later."

"Leave her be, soldier," Gordon said.

Conway didn't bother to look at him. "Go git your own squaw, farmer. Ain't you heard the yellowlegs git first pickin's?"

Willa tried to tear free and the trooper gave a jerk on her arm that almost pulled her off her feet. He started dragging her toward the door. Gordon grabbed Conway's elbow and pulled hard. It tore the man's hand off of Willa and wheeled him back toward Gordon.

Conway cursed him and swung a punch. Gordon ducked aside and Conway couldn't stop himself from lurching forward with the blow, going heavily into Gordon. Gordon knew he had to go all the way now. He grabbed the Jeff Davis hat and pulled down so hard that the pinned-up brim tore loose from the crown. Blinded, Conway made a roaring sound and reached up with both hands to tear the hat off his eyes. It exposed his belly.

Gordon put all his weight behind the blow. It doubled Conway over. It knocked the wind out of him in a bellowing wheeze and sent him staggering backward into a table. The table skidded away but he grabbed its edge and kept himself from falling. He straightened up, sucking wind, his face pinched and sick. The noise in the room had stopped. Conway shook his head, still fighting for air, and blinked at Gordon. The drunken fog was gone from the trooper's eyes. They were glittering prisms in the smoky yellow light. He made a soft sound and went for his Colt.

Gordon pulled his gun. It came into his hand, heavy, cold, aimed at Conway. The trooper's Army Colt was only halfway out of its stiff holster. He didn't try to pull it any higher. Gordon saw the surprise in the man's eyes. It was no less than his own surprise. His draw had been an automatic reaction, as thoughtless as picking up the rifle to shoot the bear. He couldn't understand how he had beaten Conway. The barkeep's voice came out of the yellow haze.

"Shoot, boy. It's your privilege."

A tremor ran through Gordon. He couldn't shoot. He just *couldn't*. It wasn't like the bear now. He had stopped to think and he couldn't shoot. He saw Conway's lips moving loosely, cursing him without sound. He wondered if the man was drunk enough to go ahead and draw anyway. If it lasted much longer his hand would start shaking with the rest of his body and the soldier would see it.

"Get out the door," he told Willa. "Get out behind me."

He heard the girl move, and started backing after her. Conway straightened.

"Careful, Conway," one of the soldiers said softly. "If he can draw like that he can shoot like that."

Gordon heard Willa open the door behind him. He backed out, and she slammed it shut. He heard a roar of voices from inside. He wheeled and grabbed her arm and ran with her toward the dark grove of trees. Once inside the shadowed cover they stopped.

"Gordon," Willa said. "Gordon—"

Her voice was shaking with reaction. She was standing close. He didn't know whether she did it or he did it, but she was suddenly in his arms. He felt the trembling of her body. She pressed her face to his chest, her voice muffled.

"Gordon—why did you do it?"

"That's a crazy question," he said. "It was the natural—I mean, I didn't think—when he hurt you, when I saw him do that—Willa, I love you, that's why I did it. I love you—"

He broke off, shocked to hear his voice saying the words. Maybe it was the feel of her body against him, soft, warm, like nothing he'd ever felt before, or the things that had been growing in him these past days, every time he looked at her, the hungers, the yearnings, the wants that he couldn't contain any longer. He didn't know.

Willa didn't seem so surprised. "I hoped," she said. "I mean I thought I saw—when you looked at me—your eyes. It is the way my mother said. A person doesn't have to decide, or think about it. I have known for a long time—I mean, about my own feelings . . ."

Over her shoulder he saw light appear in the dark doorway of the sutler's store. She felt him stiffen, and turned to look. The shape of a man lurched out.

"Gordon?" It was Blackhorn's voice. "Willa—where the hell are you?"

Gordon answered him, softly, and Blackhorn crossed to the trees. "What happened in there?" the old man asked. "That damn soldier is cadgin' drinks from everybody and blabberin' how he's acomin' after you. I got the idea he's afraid to come through the door for fear you'll shoot his lights out."

Gordon put his gun away. "Nothing. I mean—just a drunk yellowlegs."

"It don't matter," Blackhorn said. "We got better cause to skin outa here than that. The sutler said there was a man in here yesterday asking for you."

Gordon's mouth went dry. "Tom Union?"

"By the description."

"Why here? I mean, how would Union know?"

"He probably caught up with your horse down there, found it had drifted on you. Time he got back to South Pass City you was gone. Your tracks headed north, remember? It's natural he should look up here for you. I don't know what he's adoin' now. Maybe goin' on, maybe circle around and come back. Chances are you'll be gone before he shows up. The wagon train leaves for Fort Lincoln tomorrow. The sutler says you kin git a job wranglin' the stock."

Gordon stood quietly, his face stiff. Indecision was a knife in him. One side of him said he should face up to Union, to settle for that business at the dugout. Because Union was MacLane's man and MacLane was a murderer. And that tarred Union with the same brush. Yet— Thinking of the gun he had drawn so smoothly in the sutler's store put a chill through him. He could not shoot the gun. He could not kill Tom Union.

Licking his lips, he said, "If I go with the train, what about you?"

"Willa'n me, we'll head back into the Wind Rivers tonight."

"You can't! I mean—I can't leave you, Blackhorn."

"I done my part, jigger. I brung you as far as I could, kept my word to your pa."

"It isn't that. Willa—"

"What about Willa?" Blackhorn's voice was sharp.

"I won't let you take her. I mean—the way you treat

48

her, like a dog or something . . . you ain't got no right—"

"Who ain't got the right? She's my daughter. She's a squaw."

"She's a human being. She's a woman. I won't let you take her—"

"You won't what?" It came from Blackhorn in a roar.

"Blackhorn—I didn't mean it that way. Well, dammit, yes I did—" He looked at Willa, imploringly. She was a dim willowy shape in the darkness, silent, waiting. Blackhorn made a rattling sound.

"Gordon, I think I know what's on your mind. You been makin' calf's eyes at my girl too long. Now you lissen—"

"Shut up," Gordon said. He was surprised at his brashness. He'd never talked to anybody that way before. Something had changed in him. Maybe hitting the soldier had done it. As though he had grown up all in a minute. "I never got a chance to ask you," he told her. "There's probably a parson here. We could go to him tonight—right now."

Blackhorn made an explosive sound. "She ain't agoin' to no parson with you. Hark from the tomb. You think I'd let her git hitched to a jinx like you? What about Union? What about MacLane? You'll have that hangin' over your head the rest o' your life."

"It ain't that bad. We can get away, go on west—"

"Not far enough. Never far enough. Never knowin' where it'll come from, or when. Every time you walk out the door. Every town you hit. A gun waitin' in any alley. Just as liable to git her as you. I won't let you drag her into that, Gordon."

"That sounds just fine—acomin' from you."

Blackhorn slapped his head. "I can't help the way I treat her. Everybody's got his way of lovin' a thing, jigger. I guess I give her the back of my hand sometimes. But she's my daughter—"

"You haven't asked me," Willa said. "You haven't even bothered asking me what I want." It made Blackhorn stop talking and look at her. She moved beside Gordon, taking his arm. "I don't care who's after him, Blackhorn. I love him."

Blackhorn gaped at her. He turned and began to pace, rubbing the back of his neck, mumbling to himself. Gordon could only catch snatches of his talk.

"That's the way the hair turns . . . old bear . . . goin'

49

blind, rheumatism . . . cub's run out on him . . . can't count on nobody . . ." He stopped, staring at her. "You really mean it. You'd hitch up with this jinx?"

"I mean it."

Blackhorn rubbed his hand over his mouth. He seemed to look at Gordon, then turned away. He scratched his beard. He spat.

"Maybe you're jist doin' this to git away from me. Maybe . . . if I'd treated you better—"

"It wouldn't have made any difference," she said.

"Ain't there anything I can say?" he asked. She gazed at him, not answering. At last his shoulders sagged. He let out a long, wheezing breath. "I must be gittin' old. Few years ago I would have knocked Gordon on the head and dragged you off, kickin', Willa. Well, maybe I learned somethin' from the Injuns. They know when to quit fightin'. Man can't stop a buffalo stampede. Got to drift with the storm. I tell you what, Gordon. There's a parson at the fort, but Injuns ain't allowed in there. Willa an' me, we'll wait here. You fetch the parson back."

Gordon couldn't believe the old man had given up. "You mean—you're not—"

"You heard me. Jump now—afore I change my mind."

Gordon gave Willa's arm a squeeze, then turned and hurried through the trees. A pack of Indian dogs yapped at his heels as he skirted the Shoshone camp. He saw the fort beyond the camp, a shapeless mass of buildings in the darkness. As he crossed toward it the doubts began to come. He must have been crazy or something. He was only twenty. Willa was three years younger. They were just a couple of kids. No wonder Blackhorn had objected.

How could he support her? He didn't know how to do anything. A wrangler on the wagon train would get maybe fifteen dollars a month. And it was going East, not West, away from the men who had slain his parents.

He should have waited. Should have tried to learn a trade. Then he could have asked her. But how long would that take? The way he was going on, a body would think he didn't love her. That wasn't true. He did love her. The feel of her in his arms came back, the giddy yearning. They would find a way. His pa had married when he was only nineteen.

And what had happened? He thought of what his mother had suffered—the years of running, hiding, fearing—

and the way it had ended. And now the same threat hung over Gordon. And he knew he couldn't go back to Table Rock and face up to MacLane with a gun. MacLane would kill him. And right here, now, in this area was a man who answered the description of Tom Union. Tom Union hunting one Gordon Conners. Hunting him as he would a snake.

Blackhorn was right. He couldn't ask Willa to share the sort of life he'd have to live. Or was he just trying to find another way out? he asked himself.

He stopped, startled by a voice that came out of the night. It was a sentry, challenging him. He said he had come to fetch the parson. The sentry said there was no parson at the fort.

It took Gordon a moment to digest this. Then he began to understand. He should have been suspicious. The old man had given in too easy. He turned and ran back toward the trees. He could not find Blackhorn and Willa where he had left them. The grove was empty. He crossed at a run to the hitchrack in front of the store. All of Blackhorn's horses were gone, even the horse that Gordon had ridden.

Gordon got so mad he began to shake. Blackhorn had made a fool of him. For a moment he thought he was going to steal one of the other horses at the rack and go after them. But which way? It was too dark to track. They could have headed out in a dozen different directions. Sick with fury and helplessness, he stared off into the night. He wished that soldier would come out of the store. He could shoot now. He knew damn well he could.

Chapter Seven

GORDON SLEPT in the open by the river that night. He woke up so stiff he could hardly move. He knew he should keep out of sight, with Union liable to come back any time. He spent some time in the Indian camp, talking with a few Shoshones who could speak English. They could give him no idea as to which way Blackhorn might have headed.

Blackhorn had said the wagon train was leaving that morning but Gordon didn't want to go with it. He would only be going that much farther away from Willa. He tried to find some work around the fort, but most of the settlers were homesteaders, having a hard-scrabble time of it anyway. Hunger finally drove him to risk the sutler's store. He made a deal to chop half a cord of wood for a meal. In the back room of the store the sutler's wife gave him some hogside and a mess of milk, eggs, corn meal and molasses that she called white-pot. He was on his third helping when the sutler came in and said there was somebody looking for him.

Gordon turned cold. "A big jasper, so tall he can't tell when his feet are cold, riding a Crazy Moon horse?"

"No," the sutler said. "A little girl, so short a man couldn't see her in a cornfield, riding a calico mule."

Gordon found her out front, standing with Blackhorn's mule and one of the Crazy Moon horses she must have led. There was a bruise on her face and her buckskin dress was torn and he guessed what had happened immediately. He took her in his arms for a moment, holding tight, oblivious to the curious stares of the homesteaders and troopers passing in and out of the saloon. Then he thought of Tom Union and he took up the reins of the two animals and guided her toward the grove of willows.

"Blackhorn made me do it," she said. She was dusty and exhausted from the long ride and her lips were trembling. "After you started for the fort last night he twisted my arm behind me . . . hand over my mouth—I couldn't fight him, Gordon—"

"I know, I know, I figured it was like that," he said. "That old snake."

"We didn't make camp till near dawn. He tied me up. There was a sharp rock. I frayed the rope—he was asleep . . ."

Gordon led her into the cover of the trees. He dropped the reins and she came to him again. For a while he thought she was going to cry. But she made no sound. She clung to him, her face buried tightly against his chest. It made him feel like a man again. He had felt so foolish last night when he knew how Blackhorn had tricked him, so young, so confused. Now all the doubts were gone.

"We can't stay here," he said. "Blackhorn will be following."

"Not very fast," she said. "I stampeded the other horses when I left."

He pulled back, looking at her, and he couldn't help

smiling. She answered, a wistful touch of humor that deepened the single dimple in her cheek. Then he sobered.

"Willa, I did a lot of thinkin' last night. I was so mad at losin' you I was sick. But there's somethin' else. Maybe Blackhorn's right—maybe I don't have no right to drag you into this trouble—"

She stopped him with a soft pressure of her fingers on his lips. "Do you think, when two people get married, that all the trouble in the world stops?" she asked. "Do you think, if we didn't have this trouble, we would not have other trouble?"

"No. Of course not. There's my work. I mean—I don't have a trade."

"Of course. And you don't have a house. Or any money. There will always be trouble. If we let that stop us we'd never get married." She settled back, seeming to move away from him. "Maybe you've changed your mind. Maybe you want me to go back to Blackhorn."

"No, I can't let you do that."

"Gordon—do you love me?"

He took her in his arms again. He kissed her. It was strange—he had kissed other girls, it had always been so fumbling, so awkward . . . and now it felt so natural.

"Willa . . . we could catch up with the wagons. The sutler mentioned a town about a day's ride south. Lander. There must be a parson there."

And he knew in that moment that he would build a new life with her. He had a fondness for cattle. "Takin' after his Uncle Mart," his father used to say when Gordon would mention it. Uncle Mart, his mother's brother, had gone to Texas years back. There was a strain between the two families. Uncle Mart would write to Gordon and never to his sister or her husband. He would tell Gordon about the cattle business and how the only way for a man to work was from a saddle. A man who pushed a plough was almost as lowdown as the worm under a wet rock. Uncle Mart was dead, but all the things he had said were still fresh in Gordon's mind. Somehow they would make their way to Texas. He would find someone who had known his Uncle Mart. He would get a riding job. He could ride well, that was one thing he could do. And he could rope. They'd forget this north country. He would push from his mind all thoughts of vengeance. They might even take a new name so nobody could ever find them. . . .

53

The train hadn't gotten far south of Fort Washakie. There were twenty big Murphy wagons that had hauled freight on a government contract to the fort and were returning to Fort Lincoln empty. The wagon boss said Gordon could still have the job wrangling stock and Gordon got a ride for Willa on one of the wagons.

It was a long, monotonous drive, the mountains always towering on their right flank. They crossed a river called the Popo Agie and camped outside Lander in the late afternoon. Gordon had to help unhitch and herd the mules. With the animals grazing, one of the teamsters took Gordon's place while he went in for dinner. Despite the long day and the hard work, he didn't have much appetite. He saw that Willa hadn't eaten much of her food either. He got an advance of four-bits on his pay from the wagon boss and rode into Lander with Willa. It was a little one-galus town, dust caking the windows so thick they wouldn't give off any glare, dust lying in cornstarch drifts against the high curbs, dust stirred up by the slightest movement till it lay across the street in a bank of yellow haze higher than a man's waist.

There was a minister in a shake house next to the saloon, a hardshell Baptist. The minister said his usual fee was a dollar but when Gordon rang the four-bit piece on the table the man figured he could do it cut-rate seeing as how they were under-age anyway.

When they got outside the sun was setting. The shadows of the buildings lay like streaks of smoke across the street. They led their horse and the calico mule down the street toward the camp.

Gordon stole a sidelong glance at Willa. There was a faint smile of contentment on her lips.

He cleared his throat. "Uh . . . I don't feel any different."

Her face was turned away so that all he could see was the soft curve of her cheek. The dying sun seemed to give it a pink glow.

"I don't feel any different either," she said. Her fingers were tight on his arm.

"When we git back to camp . . . let's not tell 'em—not right off, anyways . . . that is, they'll want to throw a big doin's, and have dances and make an almighty whoop-te-doo—"

"We won't tell them," she said softly.

54

They were almost at the end of town and they left the road and crossed the fields toward the wagon corral. The only noise behind them was the creak of a big hay wagon pulling into town. The sound echoed shrilly against the buildings.

"Gordon," Willa said.

"Yes."

"I would like to ask something."

"Sure."

"Is it true that your people—"

"Don't say it that way, Willa. There ain't no more your people or my people. Blackhorn has got it stuck in your head that you're Indian. You're just as much white as Indian. You're whatever you want to be."

Her face was turned down. "Thank you, Gordon."

"I'm sorry. I didn't mean to interrupt you. What was you goin' to say?"

"When your—I mean when a man gets married, does he carry his wife in the door of their house?"

"Over the threshold. At least ma said pa did it."

"I would like you to do it."

"We ain't got no threshold," he said.

"A wagon tongue will do," she said. It would make me feel very married. The wedding did not make me feel very married, but I think this would make me feel that way."

Light was failing swiftly when they reached camp. Dusk was a sooty veil that made dim monsters of the wagons. A few campfires were still going but most of the teamsters were already rolled in their blankets beneath the freighters. Gordon stopped by the number two wagon.

"I don't guess we'd better sleep underneath," he said awkwardly. She didn't answer. He couldn't see the expression on her face in the dusk but he could see she was looking at him now, the solemn, unwinking gaze that had disturbed him so often before. "I put some wild hay inside," he said. "It'll make us a good bed. The wagonmaster, he loaned me a blanket."

She didn't speak. He took the reins of her mule. Her hand was warm. He hitched the horse and mule to the front wheel. His hands were trembling. He cursed himself soundlessly.

"Willa," he said, and his voice choked.

"Yes, Gordon . . ."

55

The sound of her voice was husky. It didn't sound like a little girl's voice any more. He realized how close she was standing. The scent of her crept against him, musky, wild. He reached out for her. She came heavily against him, holding his face between her hands and pulling his lips down to hers. There was a pounding in him somewhere, a strangled feeling.

"Willa," he said. "Willa . . ."

He picked her up in his arms. He carried her to the wagon tongue, and stepped across. He had thought it a silly, girlish notion when she had asked it, but now he understood what it meant to her. It changed something. It sealed something.

"I wish it was a door," he said. "I wish we were inside our house."

She clung to him tightly, her face buried against his chest. Before she could answer he heard a sound somewhere behind him. It was a clinking sound, like a bit chain, or a spur. It made him wheel. He was still turning when he saw the shadowy figure at the lowered tail-gate of the wagon.

The flash and the roar came simultaneously. Not until he felt Willa's body jerk with the bullet did Gordon realize it was a shot. The impact made him stagger backward. He tripped on the wagon tongue and fell, with Willa still in his arms. It was what saved his life. He heard the gun explode again. The bullet went through empty air where he had stood an instant before, slamming into the wagon bed behind him.

He hit hard and it dazed him. He rolled over, sprawling on Willa to protect her with his body. There was a third shot, and dirt spewed into his face.

The camp was awake now, the men shouting, scrambling from under the wagons. One of the teamsters must have seen the last gunflash. Using it for a target, he began firing. Gordon heard the shadowy figure at the tail-gate curse, saw him wheel and fade into the night. A moment later Gordon heard the sound of a running horse.

"Quit shootin'," Gordon shouted. "It's too late now!"

The teamster stopped. The greasy smell of black powder hung in the air. Gordon was on his hands and knees above Willa. He realized that when he had heard the sound and had turned, he had swung her into the path of the bullet. She had taken the shot that was meant for him.

Somebody was bringing a torch from the fire. As its wavering circle of light fell across Willa's face, Gordon could see that she was looking up at him. The front of her dress was soaked with blood. She had trouble speaking.

"Will you tell them now?" she asked.

She closed her eyes. The wagonmaster crouched beside her, looking at her tear-stained face.

"I think it's over, son," he said. He put a hand on Gordon's shoulder. It seemed a long time before he said, "What was it she wanted you to tell us?"

Gordon didn't understand how he could speak. It sounded like somebody else's voice, coming out of him. "We just got married," he said. "She's my wife."

His face was stone. His whole body was stone. He stared at Willa and slowly got to his feet. The men watched him. He saw the sign left by the murderer; Gordon walked stiffly across the campground, following the tracks until they came to a spot where a horse with trailed reins had stood, waiting while its master killed a girl.

Gordon noted the difference in the two sets of tracks. The murderer had walked, slowly, to stalk his enemy. Would-be murderer then. The tracks leading back to where the horse had stood had been made by a man running.

He followed the tracks of the horse for a dozen yards, saw where they cut toward a brushy hill. He made a mental note of the direction taken by horse and rider.

And he thought of what would happen when he faced this man, as he would. He felt a tremor along his arms and the old sickness began to churn in him. But not as strong as before. Not nearly as strong. He would face him. He would have a steady hand when he sent a bullet into the man's stomach. He wanted him to die slowly. He wanted to tell him about Willa while he died.

He walked over to one of the wagons and got a shovel and some distance from the camp he began to dig.

Chapter Eight

AT DAWN A MIST rose off the river. It fogged the bottomland timber and turned everything the color of old ashes. The crowd of teamsters seemed to float in its gray vacuum, standing silently around Willa's grave. Gordon had spent half the night burying her, and the other half sitting on a rock beside her wooden headstone. He couldn't remember what he had thought about during that time. It was a blank to him now, as he stood shivering in the mist. The same parson who had married them was reading the funeral service.

When it was over the parson tried to give Gordon some condolences. Gordon kept nodding, but he couldn't seem to concentrate on the words. He closed his eyes and wished they'd go. The parson left and the teamsters broke up and started back toward camp.

"You still coming with us, son?" the wagon boss asked.

"No."

Gordon wasn't aware when the man left. He sat on a deadfall, staring at the grave. He wished he could cry. He wanted to cry. She had looked so small and helpless, and it was his fault. He could hear the horse and the calico mule stirring nearby. The teamsters had tethered them to a tree for Gordon and they were cropping at the buffalo grass. It was a matted turf, going to seed, straw-colored from curing all summer long in the sun. He heard the creak of a saddle but did not look up, for he judged it to be one of the teamsters.

But when he did not hear the sound again he turned to see a rider at the edge of the clearing.

It wasn't a teamster. It was Blackhorn. He had one of his Navy Colts out, pointed at Gordon.

Slowly Gordon got to his feet, wondering how long Blackhorn had been sitting there. Maybe through the whole ceremony. Gordon didn't feel any surprise, or any fear. He couldn't feel anything.

"If you think I deserve killing," he said, "go ahead and drop the hammer."

Blackhorn didn't answer. He continued to hold the gun on Gordon, one twisted, rheumatic thumb hooked over the big single-action hammer. His face was half-buried in the curly red mat of his hair and beard. It looked like the mane of a mangy old lion, frosted gray, filthy with bear grease, matted with buffalo bur and wild hay and whatever else blew on the wind. The pleats in his cheeks were deep and grimy. His eyes were ice-colored, blank and glittering, a little mad. He was sitting on one of the Crazy Moon horses. The gun began to tremble in his hand

and Gordon thought he was going to fire.

Blackhorn made a broken sound. The gun sank against the saddle. He bowed his head.

"I wish I could kill you," Blackhorn said. "I wish to God I could."

Something broke inside Gordon, a wound opening up, and all his grief and guilt seemed to pour out. "I didn't have no right to take her. I just as well killed her myself. She was the best thing we ever had, Blackhorn, either of us. You treated her like dirt and I killed her. I—" His voice broke. "I guess I'm a jinx. You said I was."

"Jinx? You was born under a dark cloud. Yeah, you're a jinx to man or woman."

Blackhorn began shaking his head from side to side. It was a slow, strange movement, as though he didn't have any control over it, going on and on. He climbed off the horse, still moving his head, and leaned against the animal with his face touching the saddle. He stood there for a long time, like a man exhausted to the point of collapse. Finally he shuffled to the other end of the deadfall and sat down on the rotten tree trunk. His elbows were on his knees, the gun dangling from one hand. Gordon thought he looked a hundred years old. When he finally spoke it wasn't much more than a feeble croak.

"It wouldn't do no good to kill you," he said. "Damn you, it wouldn't do no good."

"You think it's what I deserve," Gordon said.

"She made the choice. She come back to you. The man that needs killin' is Tom Union."

"It was dark. All I saw was a shadow. A big shadow."

"Some Injuns camped yonderly said Tom Union come ridin' from this direction last night."

Gordon's mouth hardened. "Blackhorn, I want to do it."

"What?"

"Tom Union."

"You wouldn't stand a chance."

"Maybe." He gave a short laugh. His face looked older. "I figured me an' Willa would go to Texas. I had an uncle there in the cattle business. I had our life all figured out. I was goin' to forget MacLane and Union and everything that had happened to my folks. I figured to turn my back on that an' make me an' Willa a new life."

"Plans ain't no good. A man lives from one sunup to the next."

"I'm goin' back to Table Rock. I'm goin' to have a gun in my hand."

"One gunshot and you'll run for the brush."

"You can help me get over it." Gordon looked at the seamed old face.

Blackhorn held his gaze for a moment, then said, "I'll do it. For her."

It took them a day to get back to the camp from which Willa had escaped. Blackhorn had left one of the Crazy Moon horses there along with the gear. They packed the horses and headed into the Wind Rivers.

Blackhorn knew where there was an abandoned trapper's cabin. The roof had fallen in and some of the logs had rotted away. They had to make it snug before the big snow. They felled some fresh timber. Blackhorn had a froe in his gear to split the logs into puncheons and to rive shakes for the roof. They used willow sticks to patch the cat-and-clay chimney, and plastered it thickly with mud. They raised a shed for the horses out back and packed in some wild hay they cut in the lower meadows. Blackhorn killed a bear and some bucks and they made jerky by cutting the meat in strips and smoking it over a fire. After two days with his head in the smoke Gordon could understand why squaws had such bad eyes.

It was all hard work and Gordon was glad for it. He didn't have time to think about Willa, or what lay ahead for him. They finished the cabin, and were through laying in supplies, and one morning Gordon woke to see Blackhorn's bunk empty. He walked to the door and saw the old man putting a target against the deadfall across the clearing. Blackhorn crossed back to Gordon.

"We don't have too much .45 ammunition," Blackhorn said. "That tree trunk'll stop the lead and we can dig it out and reload." He crossed the room and picked up Gordon's Colt. "Might as well put in an hour before breakfast. A man ain't so sharp on a full stomach."

He held out the gun. Gordon remembered the time when' he wouldn't take a gun from his father. He let Blackhorn put it in his hand, and stood staring at it. He had known this moment would come. He had thought about it with a mixture of anticipation and dread. He had been glad he could put it off with the work, yet he had been impatient to get to it. To know if the bitterness and outrage he had felt at Willa's death were still strong enough to overcome his fear.

When Gordon didn't move, Blackhorn said, "Gordon, you want to be a hunted man all your life?" Gordon didn't answer. Blackhorn tugged peevishly at his beard. "You want to spend the rest of your life like your pa? Like me? Runnin'. Always makin' sure there's a back way out, never stayin' in one place long, gittin' the shakes every time you come to a dark alley. It's hell. I don't know how much of the runnin' your pa did was from the law, and how much was from MacLane."

"It don't matter no more whether I'm hunted or not. Nothin' matters but *her*. You're goin' to teach me how to kill."

Blackhorn gave him a long look. "Easy, boy. You're goin' up against some tough men. The toughest. Mac-Lane—"

"Yeah. The one that wrote that holdup note. Why didn't pa get rid of it all them years?"

"You goin' to git rid of it?"

Gordon didn't answer. He realized the same thing his father must have realized—it would be useless to destroy the note. The man who had written it would never be sure. His only complete safety lay in killing Gordon's father. And now Gordon.

"Either you live like a weasel the rest of your life, or you go back and face MacLane," Blackhorn said. "It's a decision you'd have to make sooner or later, even if it hadn't been for Willa."

"It's still for Willa," Gordon said.

He went outside. The target was one of the shakes they had rived, a bulls-eye drawn on it with charcoal. Blackhorn told him how to sight, bringing the gun down on the target instead of up to it. The smudge of charcoal appeared over his sights. He began to tremble with a sick dread. It wasn't any use. He would panic. He couldn't do it. He knew he couldn't do it.

He thought of Willa. He squeezed the trigger.

The crash made his eyes shut, made his body jump. The echoes sent a shattering sound through the timber. He was shaking. He wanted to run. It took a savage effort to keep from running.

"Wide and high," Blackhorn said. "You got to keep your eyes open, jigger. Let's walk closer to the deadfall.

We can't waste any more lead. Forget about aiming now. Forget about every else. Jist think about keeping your eyes open."

Stiffly Gordon walked to the fallen tree. He didn't think he could control himself again. Deliberately he tried to think of Willa again, tried to take himself back to that moment over her grave, tried to resurrect the grief, the outrage, the hate for Union. He had known he could conquer himself then. There had been no doubt in him. No fear. He kept his eyes closed until he could see her face.

He opened his eyes and began firing. His eyes tried to squeeze shut with the first shot. He kept them open. He wanted to throw the gun from him on the second shot. He held it and fired again. He kept firing till it was empty. He was drenched with sweat. His muscles kept jumping and knotting in spasms. His whole body was rigid with his fight to keep from bolting. Blackhorn took the gun from him.

Gordon stumbled to the deadfall and sat down. He held his head between his hands. He could still hear the roar of his shots. He was shaking and he thought he was going to be sick.

"Blackhorn, it's no good, I can't do it—"

"You already done it."

Blackhorn shoved the reloaded Colt into his hand. Gordon stared glassily at it. He couldn't do it again. He knew he couldn't do it again. Once more he tried to think of Willa. He had loved her. She had made him want to be a man.

He got up. He began shooting again. This time he couldn't keep his eyes open. Panic smothered him. He shouted something he couldn't understand and fired again. He held the gun in both hands to keep from throwing it and running, and kept squeezing the trigger blindly, shouting every time the gun slammed, the sound roaring through his head, hurting his ears, stopping his breath. He kept squeezing the trigger and cocking it. He didn't even know the gun was empty till Blackhorn yelled.

"That's enough, jigger. You emptied your wheel three shots ago."

Gordon heard the hammer click on an empty chamber. The shots still seemed to echo in his head. He threw the Colt down. His fists were knotted so tight he could feel the nails cutting the flesh. He didn't know if the sickness in him was panic or shame.

"Blackhorn, it's no use."

Blackhorn picked up the gun. "You can't expect miracles. You emptied this six-gun twice, without arunnin'. That's exactly twelve times as good as it used to be, ain't it?"

"Yeah. Reckon it is."

Gordon walked around the park, trying to settle down. Blackhorn dug the bullets out of the deadfall. He said most of them were too battered to use again without remolding. He made a soapstone mold and melted the lead down and ran it again. The next morning they shot again. For two weeks, every day, they shot. Gordon got to the point where he could empty the gun four times before he reached the end of his control. He couldn't sleep and had lost weight; he was so spooky he jumped every time he saw his own shadow. Blackhorn said they had better rest a spell.

"There's another part of this business," Blackhorn said. "The best shot in the world ain't worth nothin' if he can't get his gun out quick enough. I got somethin' on my mind about you. You're the nervous type. Maybe that's part of what makes you so jumpy about guns. But the nervous ones is usually the quick ones. I never seen anybody jump so quick as you when you're spooked."

"The doctor said my reflexes were too fast."

Blackhorn threw back his head and let out a braying laugh. "In this business, jigger, you can't be too fast." They were standing outside the shack, both wearing their guns. Blackhorn took off his battered horse thief hat. "When I drop this, we'll draw. Don't try to be fancy. Just pull your gun."

He held out the hat. Gordon waited, watching the man's slitted eyes. Blackhorn dropped the hat.

The Colt was in Gordon's hand before he realized he had pulled it. Blackhorn hadn't finished his draw. He stared at Gordon's gun, his lips parted in surprise. He let his gun drop back into the black holster.

"That's what happened at Fort Washakie," he said. "When I come into the saloon, jist after you'd had that fight with the soldier, they was all gabblin' about it. They thought you was Tom Horn, or Billy the Kid, or some other quick-draw artist. I didn't pay much heed then. Could be you got somethin', jigger. Could be you're a natural."

Gordon put the Colt away. "What good does it do, if

I can't shoot?"

"Plenty good. I ain't never been a gunman, but I could unlimber pretty fast in my time. If you kin beat me without practice, think what you could do with a little work."

They put in their time for a few days. When Blackhorn thought Gordon had recovered enough they went back to the shooting. It was torture. Each day Gordon thought he was at the end of his string. Each day he thought of Willa.

It seemed weeks before Gordon could empty the gun without closing his eyes. It was first snowfall before he had enough control to get one bullet out of six in the target at five feet. By the time he could shoot without jumping like a startled deer the first blizzard struck.

They were trapped in the cabin for two weeks. They got cabin fever and had a brawl and sulked in opposite corners for two days without speaking to each other, doctoring their bruises with lard and gunpowder. When the blizzard broke they went out into a frozen world and started shooting again.

Chapter Nine

IT WAS THE LONGEST winter Gordon had ever spent. For Thanksgiving they had bear steak. By Christmas they were down to jerky. Come Gordon's birthday in January all they had left was pemmican and coffee made from beans they had used for three weeks.

Gordon was twenty-one, and he had found himself. He could shoot for half an hour without breaking. He could keep his eyes open and get four out of six in his target from twenty feet. It still made him so nervous he couldn't eat afterwards. He still jumped if Blackhorn fired a gun off when he wasn't expecting it. But he thought it was time. He could get a gun out fast now and he could hold it and shoot it. He could stand up against the sound of another man's gun without losing his nerve. He told Blackhorn he wanted to go back to Table Rock.

The old man didn't think he was ready. He wanted to work a while longer, till Gordon was steadier. Gordon wouldn't wait. Blackhorn finally saw it was no use. He said he'd go along. Gordon was surprised. He hadn't expected that.

"You was right about Willa, jigger," the old man said. "She was the best thing either of us ever had. If you don't get the man who killed her, I want to."

With the first thaws they left the cabin. They had been living on roots and boiled rawhide for the last days and were as ravenous as the animals. The first thing they did was head for Fort Washakie to trade the skins Blackhorn had trapped for some decent grub. The creeks were bankful with melting snow and the yellow water roared night and day. The aspens were going to seed and the fluffy down floated on the wind, coating the streams with a cottony layer and piling up against deadfalls like drifting snow. In such a land it was hard for a man to remember his mission.

Blackhorn didn't think it would do to show up at Table Rock with two rustled Crazy Moon horses, so at Fort Washakie he traded them to an Indian for a mare and a black gelding that Gordon could ride. The black was a snuffy little horse, a couple of fingers short of fifteen hands, with so much vinegar he had to pitch five minutes every time the saddle went on. His name was Spades.

At Lander they stopped at Willa's grave. Wild flax had bloomed on it like chips of fallen sky. Gordon closed his eyes and her face appeared before him and he could feel her trembling in his arms. Wiwilla. Spirit of Spring. . . .

They moved south slowly, feeling their way. At the way station north of South Pass City they heard that the rustling fever still had not died down. Bob Conners' death had not ended the trouble.

They made their last camp before Table Rock, at a place called Washakie Rocks. It would take them the better part of a day to reach town from Washakie Rocks. They followed the stage road through the sandy, sage-grayed benchlands and topped a rise where they came abruptly upon four riders.

The men drew apart, sat their horses. They were all armed with belt gun, rifle in saddle boot. Their eyes were still and they looked over the horses Gordon and Blackhorn rode. Gordon was close enough to see the four men were astride horses branded 77 which meant they rode for the big Eastern-owned outfit west of town.

Blackhorn hissed in Gordon's ear, "Yonderly is Rin Orland. Ramrod for Seventy-Seven."

Gordon remembered the long, dark face now, the thin

65

mustache, the pale eyes. The man wore a blanket coat, the lashes hanging loose. Gordon could see the butt of a black-handled gun.

"I remember you," Gordon said to the man.

The man gave him a faint smile. "Sure. The day Mac-Lane went after your pa."

"You was with Billy Halleck."

"A sorry day," Rin Orland said, nodding. "A damned sorry day."

"Were you in on it?" Gordon said. "The killing at the dugout?"

"And if I was?" Orland said softly. The three riders with him sat their saddles stiffly. Blackhorn, to Gordon's right, was cursing under his breath.

"Shoot a bobcat," the old man whispered hoarsely, "but don't spit in his eye an' expect him to lick your hand. Bein' tough is one thing. Bein' foolish is somethin' else again."

The stiffness seemed to go out of Rin Orland's narrow shoulders. He was in his middle-twenties, and the tip of his nose was sunburned. "It was my first week in this country, Conners," he told Gordon. "When I found out what was goin' on—what MacLane figured to do, I went back to town. No, I wasn't in on it."

Gordon nodded. "I'm glad to hear it."

Rin Orland moved his horse up and halted, eying Gordon. "You've changed. You still gun shy?"

Gordon swallowed. He did not lower his gaze. "You'll know—in time."

"You'll be after MacLane," Rin Orland said. And when Gordon made no reply, he went on, "There was an inquest after the shooting, but MacLane was cleared."

"Then murder don't mean much in this country," Gordon said stiffly.

"Coroner's jury held that MacLane's boys was justified in killing your pa. Don't forget your pa killed a Crazy Moon hand. That's all the excuse MacLane needed."

"I see."

"Sorry we give you two a hard-eyed look when you rode up," Orland said easily. "But somebody around here's bein' fancy with a running iron. We look over strangers real careful."

"I suppose you'll tell MacLane I'm back," Gordon said.

Rin Orland shook his head. "I tell MacLane nothing."

66

He looked back at his three men. "That goes for you. Say nothing." He looked back at Gordon. "Good luck, Conners."

The four men rode off, dipping into a draw, the yellow dust from their passing a smudge against the clear sky.

Blackhorn removed his horse thief hat, wiped his brow. "You ain't goin' to live long, jigger, talkin' like that to a man."

"I only asked questions."

"Yeah. You asked Orland if he killed your pa an' ma. In so many words you asked him. An' if he said he had, then you an' me would've had to do some shootin'. Two against four. Them ain't very good odds, jigger."

"Maybe you better go back, Blackhorn. Back to Wind Rivers."

Blackhorn put on his hat. "I ain't scared of dyin'. I just don't believe in unlockin' hell's front door myself."

They started again and Gordon said, "Thanks for stickin' with me, Blackhorn."

"We got Willa between us, jigger."

They rode for five miles and Gordon said, "I like Rin Orland. I hope we got a friend in him."

"Remember this, Gordon," Blackhorn said seriously. "Friendship is somethin' a man earns. It don't come quick like buyin' a new hat and puttin' it on your head." He gave Gordon a long, sidelong glance. "You go through the fire together an' then you got friendship."

"Like us," Gordon said.

"Yeah. That's what I was meanin'."

In the late afternoon they came to the rise that brought Table Rock abruptly into view. Towering to the left of the road was the huge flat-topped rock and beyond it, cupped in a valley shaped like a rheumatic hand, was the town. Coal smoke hung over the buildings in a sooty black fog. It came from the four brick smokestacks at the north end of town. Gordon could see the faintly gleaming spiderweb of sidings and switchtracks spreading east from the tracks, converging finally into the single main line that ran past the long yellow station house at the corner of Main and Station Street. At the north edge of town, where Main became the stage road, the three hundred tarpaper shacks of Ricetown huddled under the overhanging rock. The Chinese lived there. They were the coolies who had been imported to put down the tracks in 1865. They had stayed on to maintain the tracks and work in the coal mines when the town was made a division point.

Gordon and Blackhorn passed through the exotic gabble of Ricetown, oppressive with the smells of incense and roast pork, garbage and decay, and reached the business district of Table Rock. Snow still clung in dirty crusts to the high curbs but the thaw had melted it in the center of the street, making a bog. Gordon planned to see Bayard first, and knew the man would probably be at his offices over the bank. It was a two-story building, the pressed bricks turned almost black by coal smoke. They left their horses at the rack. Blackhorn wouldn't go up with Gordon.

"I'm still a wanted man, you know," he said. "I'm pushin' my luck even showin' my face in this railroad town. I'll wait for you at that saloon across the way. If you come out and find me gone you'll know I had to light a shuck. We kin meet at Washakie Rocks."

A covered outside stairway led to the offices on the second floor of the bank building. There was an anteroom —dark panelling and Argand lamps and a railroad print by Currier and Ives called *Across the Continent—Westward the Course of Empire*. There were several people waiting on a hard bench and a bald cadaverous clerk behind the desk in the corner. The door behind him had a frosted glass pane, with a sign on it and gilt letters. RO-LAND BAYARD, DIVISION SUPERINTENDENT.

Gordon could hear voices from within the office, and told the clerk he wanted to see Mr. Bayard. Without looking up from his paperwork, the clerk asked in a bored voice if Gordon had an appointment.

"Tell him—" Gordon hesitated—"say it's a friend. A very old friend."

"Come back tomorrow," the clerk said without looking up.

"But I want to see Mr. Bayard. It—it's important."

"He isn't in."

Gordon felt a rush of anger, and nodded toward the closed door. "Who's doing all the talking in his office? He's in there, all right." Gordon cooled down a little. "I don't want to push in ahead of these people waiting—"

"You can't see him."

Gordon started for the door. The clerk's red-rimmed

68

eyes blinked at Gordon from behind thick glasses. He reached out one hand to slap a little bell on the desk. It tinkled and in a moment Gordon saw a big red-headed man come swiftly into the anteroom. He had a freckled face, broad, primitive, the cheeks mottled by scars. His celluloid collar cut into the swollen muscles of his neck and his shoulders were too big for his coat. It was Billy Halleck.

The man looked surprised, then grinned broadly. Gordon remembered the chalky teeth, chipped across the front by a hundred fights. One of those fights had been with Gordon. Halleck was the son of a retired railroad engineer, an old friend of the Bayards. Halleck had been one of the dozen young idlers who spent their time at the Bayard house courting Opal. On Gordon's infrequent visits there Halleck had never failed to goad him about his fear of guns.

One night Gordon had met Halleck and two of his friends on their way home from Bayard's. They were drunk and when Gordon couldn't bear their taunts any more he had fought. Halleck whipped him. Then Halleck and the other two tied Gordon to a tree and shot a gun off and Gordon had shouted until he couldn't shout any more.

"I never figured to see you again," Halleck said, looking him over. "Ain't you takin' a chance? Lots of folks hereabouts figure you was in that rustlin' with your pa."

"Maybe I came back to change their minds."

Halleck looked at the Colt on Gordon's hip. "That makes a good show. Up where folks don't know you they must have thought you was really a man."

Gordon turned red. Before he could answer, the clerk said impatiently, "This man won't believe Mr. Bayard is out."

"Get out, Conners," Halleck ordered.

Gordon shook his head. "He'll see me."

"Get out, Conners," Halleck ordered.

The clerk's red-rimmed eyes widened. "Conners," he gasped. "You mean he's son to Bob Conners the rustler—"

"The one," Halleck said, grinning. Those waiting on the bench to see Bayard were on their feet. They looked uneasy.

Gordon saw the grin on Halleck's face and it did something to him. All the misery he had known in this town seemed to focus itself on Halleck's grinning face—all the goading he had taken, the taunts, the humiliation. Mostly it concerned that day at the dugout. His parents dead. He asked the question he had asked Rin Orland: Was Halleck in on the shooting with MacLane? Just for the hell of it, perhaps.

"Maybe I busted a few cartridges that day," Halleck said. "An' if I did I done this county a favor—"

Gordon stepped forward. Halleck reached for Gordon's gun, intending to disarm him. Gordon hit him in the belly.

Halleck staggered backward into the desk. His face was loose with shock, his mouth sagging open. He made a retching sound, trying to recover. He reached beneath his coat. Gordon lunged at him, grabbing the man's wrist before Halleck could get the gun out of his underarm harness. He hit Halleck again, a slamming blow across the face. It wheeled the man aside and this time there was no desk to stop him from falling.

He hit so hard it shook the whole room. Gordon stepped over him and reached under his coat, yanking the gun out. It was a stubby Colt, one they called a Store Keeper's Model, with a three-inch barrel and no ejector. Gordon pointed it at Halleck.

"Tell me, Billy," he said harshly. "Were you in on the shooting with MacLane?"

Halleck had trouble getting to his feet. He leaned against the desk, holding his stomach. He eyed the gun. The clerk had knocked his chair over, jumping away from his desk, and his papers were scattered everywhere. There was silence in the room.

Halleck said, "No, I wasn't in on it. I was there but I didn't do any shooting."

Gordon threw the small gun across the room. He was turned so that he saw the door to Bayard's office standing open. A girl stood there, her mouth open. It was Opal.

Chapter Ten

FOR A MOMENT Gordon had a strange feeling. He wasn't in the room. He was up on top of Table Rock, alone with Opal. The corn-colored braids, the grave eyes, deep as a

70

pool. The shape of her body in crinoline now, instead of a boy's jeans and checkered shirt. Her voice was soft with shock, as she said Gordon's name. She touched her throat and looked at Halleck.

The red-headed man looked at his Colt lying on the floor across the room. But Gordon stood between Halleck and the gun. Halleck's face was dark with rage and his breathing made a strained wheeze.

Gordon took off his hat. "Maybe I should apologize, Opal. They wouldn't let me see your uncle."

"Gordon—what—where have you . . ." She trailed off, helplessly and then looked angrily at Halleck. "Billy, you should know better."

"What the hell," Halleck said. "Bayard told me—"

"Never mind," Opal said. She looked at Gordon, her eyes dark, puzzled. He thought he saw more than surprise at seeing him. Maybe he knew what was disturbing her. It disturbed him too. Seeing Halleck again had touched something new in Gordon, had triggered a violence that surprised him. Maybe Blackhorn had taught him more than he realized. Or maybe a man could be away from civilization too long.

And behind Opal now stood Bayard. And he said, his eyes mirroring his surprise, "Come in, boy, come in."

Billy Halleck picked up his gun and went downstairs. On the street he hurried up the block to the Double Deuce, the saloon in Table Rock patronized by ranchers and their riders. He squinted around the smoky room then, not seeing the man he sought, he went to the bar.

"Tom Union," Halleck said, grunting at each word for the pain at his stomach was intense. "He was here awhile ago."

"Gone upstairs," the bartender said with a faint grin. "Wouldn't do to disturb him now."

"This is more important than wimmen—"

"Not to Union, it ain't. What happened to you? You act like you run around the block with an anvil on your back."

Halleck flushed. "Just give Union this message when he comes down. Tell him Gordon Conners is back. Alive."

"Who's he?"

"Whelp of a sodbuster that the boys got rid of last year."

"Conners, huh. I remember hearing about it after I got here from Cheyenne. Kind of strong medicine, wasn't it? Killin' the woman along with her man?"

"You just give Union my message."

"Is it going to make you feel better when he gets it?" the bartender said.

"It'll make me feel one hell of a lot better."

Halleck walked out.

Chapter Eleven

THERE WERE MORE railroad prints, more dark panels, more Argand lamps in Bayard's office. Bayard stood behind an immense, ornate, gilded desk in the center of the room.

"Not a very nice homecoming for you, Gordon," Roland Bayard said. "I—I'll speak to Billy Halleck. He's a good man but impetuous at times. Good to see you, Gordon. My, my, you've grown. I don't mean in height. You're older, somehow."

"I suppose so," Gordon said. He twisted his hat in his hand. He felt awkward in the sumptuous office, out of place. It was a return of the shyness he had known with these people before. It made him realize how long it had been since he'd felt it. Then he forced it from his mind. Or tried to. He was nearly successful.

Bayard paced the room, hands locked behind him. The tails of his steel pen coat snapped nervously against the glassy polish of his Wellington boots.

"You probably wonder why I'd have a man like Halleck working for me," Bayard said. He halted his pacing. "The truth is, MacLane and his crowd gave me trouble after you left. They knew I was your dad's friend, suspected I helped you. . . ."

"I understand," Gordon said.

"Why did you come back?" Bayard asked. Then he stopped, almost apologetically. "I mean—you must have known how dangerous it would be, the feeling . . . you got away safely once—"

He thought of telling them about Willa, then decided against it. "I didn't want to be like pa," he said. "I didn't want to spend the rest of my life runnin'." He glanced at Opal.

"It's all right," Bayard said, noticing the look. "She knows the whole story, Gordon. I didn't see any point in keeping it from her, after that night."

"Yes," Gordon said. "That night. You asked me if pa had given me anything, that night. You kept asking. Were you talking about the holdup note?"

Bayard didn't answer immediately. He stood near the window. It was so thickly coated with soot that the rooftops were barely visible outside. He moistened his lips.

"Then he did give it to you?"

"How did you know about the note?" Gordon said.

"I wouldn't expect you to remember how close your father and I were, Gordon . . . you were only a few months old at the time. I was a dispatcher at Julesburg when your father was sent to prison. We took you and your mother in. You lived with us till your father escaped. Your mother took you and joined him. We lost touch after that. Until last year, when you all showed up here again. I didn't know what to do. I couldn't turn him in— I suppose it was wrong, but we'd been such close friends. I let it drag on, gave him a stake—"

"Didn't it strike you as strange that he would want to settle so close to the railroad? He couldn't help runnin' into somebody who had known him—"

"It was the only decent homestead land left," Bayard said. "A convict couldn't get clear title, a wanted man . . . the homestead was filed in your mother's name. Bob said he was sick of running . . . wanted to establish something for you, for Sarah."

"Or maybe he'd tracked his man down after all these years, and wanted to have a showdown," Gordon said. "Maybe pa had found out that MacLane was the man who planned that holdup—"

"MacLane!" Bayard said sharply.

The man's surprise was unexpected. Gordon frowned. "It don't figure any other way. You know pa didn't rustle them cows. It had to be somethin' else. Somethin' big enough to have MacLane send a man after me clear up to Fort Washakie. A man that tried to kill me. It had to be the note."

Bayard didn't answer. Lamplight made a brilliant flicker in his black eyes. He touched his silvery sideburn with an index finger. It was a habitual gesture that Gordon remembered.

"The man who planned that holdup had to be on the

inside," Gordon said. "It's why I need your help. Could you find out if MacLane was working for the railroad at the time?"

"I suppose so," Bayard said. "I can wire Omaha. They can look up the old payroll records. If MacLane was on the books it will appear."

"And then we can get a sample of his handwriting," Gordon said. "If it matches the writing on the note— that's what he was so afraid of."

"You keep talking about the note," Bayard said. "None of this will do any good unless we have it."

"I have it."

"Then you'd better give it to me. I'll lock it up in the safe."

"I'll keep it."

"What?"

"I said I'll keep it."

"Gordon, don't be a fool. You must realize how dangerous it is—like carrying a loaded bomb. Your father is dead because of it. If MacLane is still after it—"

"Roland, somebody is already dead because I shared too much with them."

"But, the town is full of MacLane men," Bayard said. "I won't let you walk out of here with that thing in your pocket. Give it to me, I insist."

"And I refuse."

A flush came to Bayard's heavy jowls. He started to say something else, then checked himself, glancing at Opal. She had been standing near the desk, watching them soberly. Bayard's substantial weight settled. He took a heavy breath.

"Very well, Gordon. Have it your way." He paused. "Where are you staying? You're welcome at our place."

Gordon shook his head. "Thanks. It would just be another risk I couldn't ask you to take. How about the homestead? Don't I inherit it?"

"You can check with the land office. I don't think you've been gone long enough to lose it by default. If you need any supplies, put them on my bill at Harper's Mercantile. Check with me tomorrow. We might have something from Omaha by then." He shook his massive head, frowning at the floor. "MacLane. The more I think of it the more it seems to make sense."

"Roland . . ." Gordon stopped, trying to find the words to express himself. Then, lamely, he said, "Thanks."

Bayard smiled warmly, crossing to put a hand on Gordon's shoulder. "Your dad and I were very close, Gordon. We'll follow this through to the end."

Gordon started for the door and Bayard said, "Remember this, Gordon." The smile was gone as Gordon looked around. "The rustling isn't over. Anvil, that English-owned outfit has been hit hard. So has Seventy-Seven."

"I met the foreman today. Rin Orland."

"A gunfighter, Gordon. A very tough man. Stay clear of him."

"How about MacLane's outfit? Have they been hit by the rustlers?"

Bayard touched his sideburn. "I don't know, Gordon. MacLane doesn't talk much."

"Rustling is like a fever. Maybe MacLane rustled his own Crazy Moon cows and planted them at our place. And the idea sort of took hold. And now he's turned on his neighbors."

Bayard spread his well-kept hands. "Could be, but Sheriff Simms has found no evidence of that."

"The sheriff couldn't find his way in moonlight with a bulleye lantern tied to his head."

"You seem bitter, Gordon," Bayard said.

"Yeah. Reckon I am."

Opal told her uncle she was going back home, and would leave with Gordon.

Outside, in front of the bank building Opal halted. She looked up at his taut features. "Gordon, you've come back for revenge."

"Maybe."

"You liked hitting Billy Halleck. I see it now. I have a feeling you would have killed him if he said he was a party to that shooting at the dugout—"

"Opal, you don't understand. My ma and pa layin' there. And—their blood on my hands."

"You've changed, Gordon." She touched his holstered gun with the tip of a forefinger. "You've conquered your fear of guns, haven't you?"

He nodded. "I can stand up to the sound of a gun without goin' to pieces."

"Don't change, Gordon. Don't change too much." She touched his arm with her gloved hand. "If MacLane is guilty he should pay for it. But not by destroying you."

"You might as well know somethin', Opal. I—I was married."

Her mouth slowly opened and she took her hand from his arm. She seemed speechless.

"An Indian girl up at Lander," Gordon went on; it hurt him to talk about it. "On our wedding night Tom Union killed her. I was holding her in my arms and Mac-Lane's man killed her."

She made a soft little sound in the shadows. "Gordon, I didn't realize. I'm so—so sorry."

"You still think revenge is wrong?"

"Yes. You stand no chance against them. They'll kill you."

"Not now they won't kill me—" He broke off as a shrill voice shouted:

"There he is, Tom! By the bank, yonder!"

Gordon wheeled, thinking the voice belonged to Billy Halleck, but not at all sure. Through the shadows he saw the immensely tall man, a head taller than anyone else on the street. Gordon saw the hard hat with the curled brim, the chaw of tobacco making its shiny bulge in one cheek, the undershot jaw puckered with old smallpox scars.

"Gordon," Opal said, frightened. "It's Tom Union."

"Get back," Gordon said hoarsely. "Get back, Opal."

He heard the sharp rustle of her dress at his side. He lost consciousness of her, of the men breaking now along the walks as they sensed trouble. Somebody shouted. Gordon saw only the tall man standing now in the center of the street. Lamplight spilling from storefronts made a yellow flash against Union's eyes as they fell on Gordon.

Gordon had thought about it over a hundred campfires. He had even dreamed about it in his sleep sometimes. He had thought it could only happen one way. There hadn't seemed any other possibility. It would be as automatic as it had been with the bear, with the yellow-legs, at the fort, with Billy Halleck. Something over which he had no control. He would see Union and he would remember Willa and he would pull his gun and shoot.

Chapter Twelve

But now Gordon knew it wasn't going to be so simple, this facing up to Union. The man hadn't made a move. And because no move had been made there was time for that breathless, suffocating feeling to move insidiously through Gordon.

It couldn't be. He had waited too long for this. Worked too long. Trained himself, tortured himself. He remembered all the other times with guns; the trapped feeling, the clammy palms, the panic, so close to the surface.

And now angling across the street, apparently oblivious to the tense scene was Adam Chaney, Bayard's brother-in-law.

"Gordon," he said, not seeing Union. "Gordon Conners." The man still wore his cranberry-red fustian, the same coat he had thrown over Charlotte Bayard's chair that night to keep Gordon from smearing the plush with his blood and grime. The fustian was incongruous with faded blue work shirt and denims shoved into half boots. Everybody had always wondered how he managed to make a living on his small Double X ranch. With his parchment-colored face and his distant eyes, Gordon had always thought a body might take him for a scholar or a parson. Until they saw his hands. They didn't match his face. They were big hands, with knobby knuckles and bulges of hard muscle alongside the thumb and old callouses still ridging the palms at the base of the bony fingers. Somewhere, a long while back, the man had done his share of work.

"Gordon," Adam Chaney said, as he came on, "I was on my way to see Roland. How fortunate you're here—" Then he sensed what was going on. He halted, turning his distant eyes on Tom Union. Adam Chaney was about a dozen yards from Union. Tom Union didn't look around at him.

The sound of Roland Bayard's voice behind him startled Gordon. The voice was strained and husky. "Opal —for God's sake—get out of the way."

Gordon did not dare turn his head. He knew Bayard had come down from his second-floor office and was now in front of the stairway.

Opal did not move. Gordon felt sweat break out from under his hat brim. His body began to shake. For a moment he thought of edging aside to get clear of Opal. But he realized it would be too risky. His first move might make Union shoot.

"Opal," he said, his lips barely moving, "you've got to —get clear, get clear!"

"No!" There was something close to hysteria in her

voice. "I can't, Gordon—I can't let you—"

Gordon saw Union shift his quid of tobacco to the other cheek, still chewing. There was a crowd gathered in front of the saloon across the street where Blackhorn had gone. Up the street, men were drifting out of the Double Deuce.

"Opal," Gordon said. "Get out—run!"

He heard Opal gasp and start struggling, and knew that Bayard had grabbed her, trying to pull her back into the stairway. It was too late.

The motion of Union's jaws had stopped.

Adam Chaney came into Gordon's vision then, walking until he blocked Gordon off from Union. He stopped, his back to Gordon, facing Union.

"Don't do it, Union," Adam Chaney said.

Union didn't answer. He began edging to one side, so he could see Gordon again. Chaney moved to keep him blocked off. "You're being a fool, Union," Chaney said. "He's no hand with a gun. There are a hundred witnesses, at least. It'll be murder. Don't do it here! Later—"

Union stopped. Chaney blocked him off and Gordon couldn't see him. And then Union turned abruptly and walked back up the street and disappeared into the crowd in front of the Double Deuce.

Gordon turned to Opal. Bayard had her by the arms and was shaking her angrily, as he would a child.

"Why did you do that?" he asked savagely.

She was close to tears. "I didn't think Union would shoot—I mean, with me there—"

"Opal," Gordon said, "he's a killer."

"I couldn't let you become one too!" Opal sounded shrill, hysterical. "Or be killed—" She broke, putting her face in her hands, sobbing, "Oh, Gordon, I don't know why I did it, don't you understand? Please . . ."

Chaney had crossed to them. He put his arm around Opal. "You shouldn't be too hard on her," he told both of them. He looked at Gordon. "She probably saved your life."

The tension swept out of Gordon. He felt sick with reaction. "I'm sorry," he said. "I guess you both thought you were doing the right thing. You took quite a chance yourself, Adam."

"He wasn't after me," Chaney said, his ague-colored face somber.

Bayard was gray at the jowls. "You wanted to see me, Adam?" And before the other man could answer, said, "Come to the house. I—I've had quite enough for one day."

The crowd had drifted up, watching them curiously. Opal was weeping quietly. She dried her eyes. "Come and see us, Gordon. Please. And—and be careful."

Gordon watched her walk away with Bayard and Chaney. He realized he wasn't the only one who had changed. He remembered how coy and frivolous Willa had made Opal seem. Now he wondered when he had ever seen that in her.

Gordon, keeping one eye in the direction Union had gone, hurried across the street to the saloon Blackhorn had indicated. The evening shift was just coming off and the place was filling up with sooty coal miners. Gordon saw Blackhorn at the end of the bar talking to a pudgy little man in a green beaver hat and a frock coat with the tails snipped off. As Gordon came up behind them Blackhorn was talking drunkenly.

"Thimblerig, you ain't roping in the suckers, now. This is Blackhorn you're talkin' to. No setup is that easy to crack. There must be a joker in the cards somewhere."

Thimblerig put a pudgy hand on Blackhorn's shoulder. "You know I wouldn't cold deck an old friend, Blackhorn. No joker, I swear, no joker. The primest stock in the country, and a buyer that'll pay a thousand dollars, meet you anywhere you say—"

Gordon halted at Blackhorn's shoulder, and the little man stopped talking. Blackhorn turned. His lips were slack and wet, in the wiry mat of his beard, and his eyes were glazed with liquor. He chuckled roguishly and introduced Gordon to Thimblerig.

"We're old pards," he told Gordon. "If I'm the greatest horse thief in the world, Thimblerig's the greatest con man. A thousand tricks, Gordon. A million games. But be careful when he's abuyin' the likker. He's always got a joker up his sleeve when he's abuyin' the likker."

"He's already bought you too much," Gordon said.

"Don't you want in on the deal?" Thimblerig asked innocently.

"Not your deal," Gordon said.

Thimblerig pouted. Three little thimbles appeared in his hand. He put them on the bar and slipped a dried pea under one. He mixed them up.

"Find the pea, gentlemen, find the pea, I take no bets from blind beggars, two-headed cowhands—"

"Or horse thieves with red beards," Gordon said. He gave a jerk on Blackhorn's arm that brought the man lurching after him. "Come on, old man," Gordon said. "We've got enough trouble in our poke already."

He took Blackhorn out the alley door. In the deep shadows there he told the old man what had happened. When he finished Blackhorn swore softly. He seemed suddenly sober.

"I seen some fellas rush outa there, but I never paid no mind. I was so busy jawin' with Thimblerig an' pourin' the first decent whiskey down my gullet in six months—" He caught Gordon by the arm. "Why didn't you yell for me, jigger? Why didn't you yell for ol' Blackhorn?"

"You better keep your nose outa the whiskey jug till Union's dead and buried. MacLane too, for that matter."

They started walking along the alley, littered with tin cans. At the corner of the saloon, Blackhorn halted, peered at Gordon.

"Could you have done it, jigger?" he said softly. "If the gal and that Chaney fella hadn't been there? Could you have drawed and shot Tom Union between the eyes?"

"I could have done it, Blackhorn." He was silent a moment as a flat bed wagon and team threw a shadow across the mouth of the alley. "I learned something today, old man."

"What's that you learned?"

"I learned there's a time for guns. I used to hate 'em. I couldn't understand pa always wantin' me— Well, never mind about that. But I know now that a man's got to fight. Opal's life was in danger tonight. I'd have killed the man that brought harm to her."

Blackhorn gave him a sharp look. "You forgot Willa already?" His voice was cold.

"I—I've known Opal a long time. Before I knew Willa, I always thought she was top of the ladder and I was grubbin' around in the dust at the bottom run. Now—"

"Now?" Blackhorn said quietly.

"Now I got to kill. And when I do she'll hate me."

"I think you gone soft, Gordon. You better leave Tom Union to me. If this gal talks soft maybe you won't figure Willa is worth avenging—"

"Don't say that again, Blackhorn," Gordon said, and walked to where they had left their horses.

Blackhorn caught up with him outside of town. The stars were clear overhead and a moon put faint light on distant hills.

"Don't pay no mind to me, jigger," Blackhorn said. "A man's got to live his life. He's got to look ahead. Weepin' on Willa's grave won't help none. . . . So you figure ol' Tom Union would have his toes curled up now if it wasn't for that gal buttin' in—"

"I told you, didn't I!" Gordon shouted. He swung out of the saddle. He was trembling and felt the cold sweat dampen his forehead.

When Gordon was back in the saddle again, Blackhorn said gravely, "I hope I taught you good, jigger. I hope I taught you good."

Chapter Thirteen

IT WAS BLACK as midnight when they reached the dugout. They approached cautiously and some distance from Gordon's former home, they quietly studied the layout. But nothing moved, there was no sign of ambush. The door to the dugout was open, half torn off its rawhide hinges, and glass from the smashed window still littered the floor. This much Gordon saw by the light of a flickering match. Gordon found one of his mother's bowls on the shelf and made a Betty lamp. He filled the bowl with creeksand, soaked the sand with fat, and stuck a rag wick in it.

The uncertain light filled the room, bringing its memories. He thought he could see a stain, where his dying father had lain by the window. His mother's calico apron still hung from a peg in the wall. He realized he had never really known his people. He had lived with them every day of his life, yet he had lived in a different world.

All he could remember of his mother was the work, the sewing, the cooking, the washing, the cleaning. He tried to picture her at something else, and couldn't. There had been times when he hated his father. He had felt guilty for it, and thought his loneliness was a punishment. A strange, silent, bitter man, suspecting anyone who didn't share his love for the soil. Gordon thought he understood some of that bitterness now. He felt bowed by a deep sadness.

By the light of the makeshift lamp Gordon saw that there were pockets dug in the sod walls, and there were scooped-out places in the floor. Gordon took the lamp to the door and peered outside. He could see where someone had been digging in the yard. Someone who had come here after the carnage and dug frantically, by the looks of things. Dug for the letter, of course.

"Damn my addled head," Blackhorn said. "A man gits to jawin' an' fillin' his gut with forty-rod so's he can't think straight. Jigger, you better put out that lamp. Light will sometimes scare off night-prowlin' varmints. It don't scare off the two-legged kind."

"I'm going to look around outside," Gordon said.

He went out and over the hummock where the dugout was built. All around the place he could see the shallow holes. He saw a broken shovel and set the lamp down and went over to pick up the shovel and see if there might be some identifying mark on it.

The lamp behind him suddenly exploded. As Gordon flung himself flat bits of crockery stung his legs. There came the far-off crack of a rifle. He lay prone and waited for the shuddering fear to envelope him. It did not come.

Blackhorn's voice reached him from the dugout, "You all right?"

"Yeah." Gordon had not been touched by the bullet. Also he had not been touched by panic.

In the distance there was the sound of a horse being ridden rapidly northward.

Blackhorn crept out, rifle in hand. "Only one of 'em," the old man said, peering into the darkness. "If I'd had brains where the whisky is I wouldn't have let you light that lamp."

"I'm learnin'," Gordon said. "I'm learnin' how it feels to be hunted. Always have a back way out of your house. Sit with your back to the wall. Poor pa. I know what he went through all them years."

"Let's forget about the letter, jigger," Blackhorn said. "Let's do our job on Tom Union for Willa's sake. Then we'll head back to the Wind Rivers—" Gordon stood in the darkness beside the shattered lamp, saying nothing. And Blackhorn said, after a moment, "Or mebbe you want to stay here on account of that gal."

There was venom in the old man's voice that Gordon did not miss. "I got no time for females," Gordon said. "But this is my home." He waved a hand at the dugout below them. "Ain't nobody goin' to run me off."

"You ain't no sodbuster like your pa."

"I'll run cows like my Uncle Mart did in Texas."

"You couldn't run five head on the land you got."

"I'll start with five, then. I'll grow. I'm not goin' to run like pa did. I won't run." His voice was shaking.

They led their mounts to a thicket some distance from the dugout, stumbling across the furrows Bob Conners had ploughed. Gordon went to sleep dreaming of Opal. And once he woke up, thinking of Willa. It wasn't fair, he told the image of Willa in his mind, for him to think of another woman. It was disloyal to Willa. But hard as he tried he couldn't regulate his dreams so that they did not include Opal.

In the morning Gordon crossed to the spot where the lamp had been shattered. Sunlight touched the broken pieces of crockery. Gordon peered in the direction the shot had come.

"If that was Tom Union out there last night," he told Blackhorn, who had tramped up behind him, "I figure he'd have tried more'n once."

"Maybe whoever it was just figured to scare you out. An' not kill you."

Gordon walked down the slant to one of the holes that had been dug in the yard. He saw the broken shovel that had caught his attention last night. The handle had been snapped in two with the pressure of the digging. Burned in the handle, probably with a red hot nail, was the brand 77.

Gordon and Blackhorn exchanged glances. The old man ran a horny thumb over the brand burned in the wood.

"Somebody from Seventy-Seven was over here diggin'," Blackhorn said. "Or else they stole a shovel."

"Which ain't likely," Gordon said. "I aim to ask Rin Orland about it next time I see him."

That morning Gordon filled in the holes that had been dug in the floor of the sod house.

"I always wanted to live in a sod house," Blackhorn said sourly. "Muddy water drippin' in the soup, gophers poppin' up through the floor, smoky as the inside of a peace pipe."

"Yeah," Gordon agreed. "It's a great life."

Blackhorn squinted at him. "Last night you talked about stayin' on here. Livin' here. You think you can kill Tom Union an' MacLane an' just figure everybody will forget about things? Hell no, you can't. They'll have you hangin' higher'n a Sunday cloud."

Gordon stood in the open doorway, smelling the resin given off by the big sticky cottonwood buds. He remembered how he had hated ploughing. How many times had his pa whipped him when he'd talk about the cattle business and his Uncle Mart in Texas. How many times had his pa laid the blacksnake to him when he refused to take a rifle and go out and kill a deer? Gordon dropped a hand to the gun riding at his hip. Things had changed. It was not a deer he was after now. It was a man. Two men. Tom Union, for what he had done to Willa, and the part he had played in the grim business here at the dugout. The other man was MacLane and he'd pay for what he'd done to Bob and Sarah Conners.

"Takes money to make a go of the cow business today," Blackhorn observed. "You got no money, you got no land to speak of. You got no beef."

"What do you want me to do?" Gordon asked over his shoulder. "Take up horse stealin'?"

Blackhorn chuckled. "There are worse trades. Think how pure you'd look alongside a murderer."

That day they had no visitors. They were running low on food. When darkness came they rolled up in their blankets some distance from the sod house. Gordon slept poorly that night. He had the dream about being locked in the room again, with his father shooting off the gun. He must have been yelling because he came awake with Blackhorn pounding on him. He finally got to sleep again.

The next morning Opal came by in her piano box wagon. Gordon remembered the short green cloak, the muslin waist and bustled skirt, the sunbonnet stiff with potato water starch. They didn't remind him so much of a school ma'arm now. Somehow he didn't feel so subdued in front of her.

"I thought you'd come and see me," she said, as he helped her down.

When he said nothing, she went on, "Gordon, I'm going to take a job. Oh, it isn't much, but I'm good with a needle and I'm going to help Mrs. Anderson at the Ladie's

Shoppe. I— Since I've been out of school, the Bayards have wanted me to stay with them. Aunt Charlotte doesn't think it proper for a lady to work but, well, sitting around the house all day, knitting samplers, collecting Bohemian glass, the latest pattern in Godey's. . . ." She made a face. "Maybe I wasn't meant to be a lady. I have to defy my Aunt Charlotte and do something with my life. I tell you this, so you will come and see me. I may move to town if Aunt Charlotte disapproves too strongly—"

"Opal, you got to stay away from me. That was a fool thing you did in town."

"I kept you from killing a man."

He shook his head. "You only put it off."

He saw the shock in her eyes and she caught his arms and tried to shake him. "Gordon, listen to me. I—I can't stand to hear you talk like a cold-blooded killer. Go to the sheriff—"

"It'd be my word against Union's. They'd believe Union."

She turned loose of him and stepped back. "I remember the boy who used to come to Table Rock. He was a dreamer. We'd talk and I thought he was the most wonderful—"

He made a cutting motion with his hand. "I'm not that boy now, Opal. He's dead. He was a fool. Everybody called him that fool Conners kid. Empty-headed. Lives in the clouds, they said."

She put a hand to her eyes and they stood in silence a moment while Blackhorn, his face bitter, watched them from the shattered window of the sod house.

"I guess I didn't mean much to you," Opal said. "I mean our—our closeness. Our talks."

"Meetin' you at Table Rock was all I lived for."

"Yet you went away. You married."

"I thought I was never comin' back. I was goin' to Texas an' look up friends of my Uncle Mart's. I—" He gave a shaky laugh. "That's how much good it does you to dream. My wife's dead. I'm goin' to kill the man who did it."

She backed to the piano box wagon. "We won't see each other again, Gordon, if you talk like that."

"It's best we don't." He did not look at her.

"I came out here to give you a message from Uncle Roland." She told him that Omaha had returned Roland Bayard's wire this morning. There had been no Rodger

MacLane on the payrolls during the tracklaying. But Gordon wasn't disheartened. He said there were thousands of men on the track crews. Half their names probably didn't appear on the books. Opal reminded him that the holdup could only have been planned by someone in a fairly important position. Such a man would certainly appear on the books.

"Then he's using a different name," Gordon said. "It's got to be something like that."

Opal tucked her lower lip under her teeth, frowning thoughtfully. Gordon remembered the habit. It had always made him think of a little child concentrating.

"You'd let me go, wouldn't you, Gordon? Out of your life. And never even lift your little finger."

"I don't want you to go, Opal. Can't you understand that? But you bein' with me is—is too dangerous."

She tried again. "If you will come with me to Uncle Roland and tell him the story about your wife's death—Well, you have to admit my uncle does have influence in Table Rock. He could see that the sheriff arrested Tom Union."

"I got to do it my way."

With a sob Opal climbed into the wagon, refusing Gordon's hand. She slapped the reins and the piano box wagon went bouncing back along the road to town, dust streaming up behind it in a yellow cloud.

When Gordon went back inside the sod house Blackhorn refused to speak to him. He said no word to Gordon for the rest of the day or night.

The next morning Gordon could stand Blackhorn's silence no longer. It was worse in a way than when they had gotten cabin fever during the blizzard. Then it had just been a case of two men being cooped up together for too long a period. Then there had been a mutual sharing, a common goal. Now Blackhorn went around grumbling like a wounded bear.

Gordon faced him over the breakfast fire. "You overheard what I told Opal. I did like Opal a lot. I still like her. But I—"

"Yeah," Blackhorn said, giving him a mean look. "You told Opal you never figured to come back here. So you took second best. My Willa."

"It wasn't that way at all," Gordon said. "I loved Willa. Damn it, I married her, didn't I."

86

Blackhorn got up from where he had been squatting beside the fire. "I'm agoin' to town. I told Thimblerig to keep his ear bent in the right places. Mebbe he'll have some news about your friend MacLane." He shot Gordon a wicked glance. "Seems MacLane is your prime interest."

Gordon caught his arm. "Listen to me, Blackhorn. First it's goin' to be Tom Union for what he did to Willa. When that's over I'll go after MacLane."

"That gal will soft-talk you out of it." Blackhorn shuffled over to where his mount was staked out. "Be back tonight. If me an' Thimblerig don't drink the town dry."

"You shouldn't go alone. And I don't like that Thimblerig."

"I don't like some of your friends, neither," Blackhorn said, and Gordon knew he meant Opal.

When Blackhorn had ridden off Gordon stood for perhaps a quarter of an hour in the yard that was pocked by the holes dug by some searcher. He was alone now. He felt Blackhorn had deserted him. Blackhorn couldn't understand that a man can love two women. Gordon didn't understand it himself, but it was fact. But he knew he had lost Opal as he had lost Blackhorn. Gordon knew his first loyalty lay to Willa. After all, she had been his wife.

He felt a stinging at his eyes as he thought of her. Some of the recently acquired hard core in him melted a little. And he felt the return of an old and familiar fear. He closed his eyes and could hear the thundering of his father's gun in his ears.

He thought of how Tom Union had looked in town, tall, the hard hat tilted forward. The big gun at his hip. At that time Gordon knew he could have drawn against Union and he felt he could beat him. Had it not been for Opal's interference. Opal's and Adam Chaney's.

Gordon remembered how Chaney had turned his back on him. How he had faced Tom Union. What had passed between the pair, unseen by Gordon? A secret signal of Chaney's words. "Not here, Union. Later." He thought that was what Chaney had said.

He gave a quick shake of his head, as if to clear it. God, he was getting suspicious of everybody. His course was plain and there was no use cluttering it up with a lot of speculation. He had to find Union. The place to look was MacLane's Crazy Moon outfit.

He removed his father's blood-stained wallet with the

incriminating letter and hid it under a flat rock.

He had just saddle Spades when he saw three riders crossing Stirrup Creek. One man was a stranger to Gordon, but he recognized the other two. Sheriff Murphy Simms—and Rodger MacLane.

Gordon stood with his hand by his gun, waiting for them. MacLane was a broad man, heavy in the saddle. Fifty years of wind and sun had stained his face the color of tobacco. He wore an old-fashioned hat with a Texas crease and his longhorn mustache nearly hid his mouth. He had never converted his six-gun from cap-and-ball and in a time when most range men were wearing Levis and other store-boughts he still wore a homespun shirt and britches of linsey-woolsey. He stopped his Copperbottom ten feet from Gordon. The horse fiddled in the dust while MacLane crossed his hands on the apple horn and leaned heavily against them.

"You got a lot of gall, comin' back," he said. He had a wheezing, asthmatic voice.

Gordon drew his gun and thumbed back the hammer and the sudden move took all three men by surprise. "You killed my folks," Gordon said in a small tight voice.

Sheriff Simms was the first to recover. "Put it up, Conners. I'm warnin' you!"

Gordon shifted his gaze to Simms, small, dried by the same sun that had colored MacLane's face. You always had the feeling that if somebody picked Simms up by the back of his neck and shook him his bones would rattle. He wore a big star on his vest and carried a gun nearly as thick at the grips as his wrist.

"You let MacLane kill my folks," Gordon accused the sheriff.

"Put up that gun," Simms ordered. "I ain't tellin' you again."

Gordon holstered the weapon. MacLane had been sitting his saddle, staring, his lips parted behind the screen of mustache. He seemed awed. "You was always gun shy," he wheezed.

Gordon ignored it. "Why didn't you bring your whole crew, MacLane? You could have trapped me in the dugout like you done my ma an' pa."

"Ease up on the rope, Conners," Simms said. "There might be a lot of feelin' against you, but if MacLane could take any legal action I would've been out here with a warrant before this."

"Warrant for what?" Gordon said.

"There's plenty of wide-loopin' been goin' on," Simms said. "Everybody's been hit."

"How about you, MacLane?" Gordon said. "You been hit too?"

MacLane's heavy face flushed. Before he could answer, Simms cut in, "You got no right to accuse a man. Your pa killed one of MacLane's riders when all MacLane wanted to do was talk to your pa."

"Talk? That's a damn lie!" Gordon's face was white. "I was there! I heard! Sure there might've been a man killed. But what would you do if somebody started blastin' your house? Just sit an' take it an' not shoot back?"

"One thing I wouldn't do," Simms said coldly, "is tuck tail an' run out on my folks. Like somebody I know did."

Gordon felt his face collapsing. The three men watched him and he thought he saw MacLane's lips form a smile but because of the brushy untrimmed mustache he couldn't be sure.

Sheriff Murphy Simms waved a thumb at the third rider, an enormous man with a network of purple veins in his bulbous nose and sweat glistening in the creases of his fat face.

"This here is Tiny Ware," Simms said. "He runs an outfit up on Bitter Creek. Last week he bought some stock from MacLane. They was bein' held in MacLane's upper pasture with a guard on 'em."

He took a piece of paper from his pocket, handing it down to Gordon. It was a bill of sale made out to Tiny Ware. It was for twenty Crazy Moon horses, describing each one in detail.

Tiny Ware had a squeaky voice. "When me and my riders come down today, all we found was the Crazy Moon guard. Somebody'd hit him on the head last night and took the stock. We lost the tracks in the badlands."

Gordon was still reading the bill. "Why come to me?"

"You're the only rustler we're sure of," MacLane said. "The only one we know."

Gordon felt his face growing hot. "That's better than bein' a murderer."

"Your pa brought it on himself," MacLane wheezed. "He could've had a fair trial."

89

"You always start your trials with a shootin'?"

"Tom Union did that," MacLane said. "Against my orders. I fired him the next day."

"Union ain't working for you now?" Gordon said in surprise.

"He ain't worked for me since that day," MacLane said. Gordon looked questioningly at Simms. The sheriff nodded. MacLane said angrily, "If your pa hadn't started shooting, I could've controlled the rest of my boys. After he killed one of 'em it broke hell loose."

Gordon had come to the bottom of the bill of sale. There was an X, and underneath it the barely legible signature of the Crazy Moon foreman, Shad Colton.

"What's this X here?" Gordon asked.

"It's my sign," MacLane said.

"When did you start signing things this way? When you realized my pa had that note you'd written?"

"What note? What in hell are you talking about? Give me that bill!"

"Son," Tiny Ware told Gordon, "you better slack off. You're the one on the griddle today, not Rodger. There ain't no shame in not bein' educated. Rodger's got to be a heap bigger than most men who could read and write. You're just lucky if you got some schoolin'. The part of Texas Rodger and me come from, they wasn't a school in two or three hunnert miles."

Gordon stared blankly at MacLane. "You mean you can't write?"

MacLane's voice shook with rage. "Damn you, Conners, what's the difference? That don't have nothing to do with rustled stock."

Gordon looked at Ware. "You came up from Texas with MacLane?"

"We brought our herds up together—just after the rails hit Table Rock."

"And MacLane didn't get here ahead of you? He wasn't up here the year before?"

"How could he be? He was in Texas the year before."

"I've had enough of this," MacLane roared. "Conners, where were you last night?"

Gordon was staring emptily at the bill of sale. He felt kicked in the stomach. MacLane sidled his Copperbottom against Gordon, tearing the piece of paper from his hand.

"I said where were you?"

Gordon looked up at MacLane. He felt exhausted. He felt empty. He ached all over and wanted to go some place and lie down and quit thinking. He didn't ever want to try to figure anything out again.

"I was here last night," he said.

The three men looked at each other. Sheriff Simms said, "We're goin' to have a look around, Conners. If we find anything you're comin' back to town with us."

"Go ahead—look."

Ware and MacLane rode off toward the creek. Simms stayed behind.

"I hear you an' Tom Union almost had it in town," the sheriff said.

"Yeah. Almost."

"Table Rock is a railroad town. Most everybody there depends on the railroad for his living. The cattle outfits, big as they are, take second place now."

"What're you gettin' at?"

"Just this. A gunfight is one thing. If you kill Tom Union without givin' him a chance— Well, chances are the jury will be made up of railroad workers. They don't give much of a damn for your kind. You'll hang, Conners. Think it over. There's worse things than bein' shot to death in a sod house. Hangin' by your neck in the jail yard with half the county lookin' on is a pretty poor way to die."

"Tom Union killed my wife! You heard MacLane say that Union started the shootin' here that day! He's a killer three times over. My pa, my ma and my wife! Goddam it, arrest him!"

"Hold on there, Conners!"

"You come out here accusin' me of rustlin' Crazy Moon horses. You don't give a damn that three good people are dead. And you tell me if I go after Union I'll hang."

"Simmer down now—"

"I suppose if Union kills me, it'll be a holiday in town."

Simms leaned over the horn. "Bein' sheriff ain't exactly the best job in the world. But the folks elected me an' I do my duty. You can't take a man to court without evidence. Why, you know that Chaney would likely hire a high-priced lawyer and get Union off, no matter what he done. Roland Bayard would do just about anything Chaney says. After all, Bayard's wife, Charlotte, is a

91

pretty demanding woman. She's not goin' to deny her own brother financial help if he shouts for it. An' between you an' me Adam Chaney couldn't live off them sections he's got out there at Double X. He dresses good. He lives good. His brother-in-law pays the bill if you ask me."

Gordon finally found his voice. "You mean Adam Chaney and Union are—friends?"

"Never said that. But Union's been workin' for Chaney ever since MacLane fired him."

Gordon was still standing with his mouth open when Ware and MacLane rode back and reported they had found no sign of rustled stock.

The three of them cut for town at a canter. And when they were out of sight Gordon spurred Spades in the direction of Adam Chaney's small spread.

Chapter Fourteen

THERE WAS NOTHING pretentious about Adam Chaney's place. The house was built of unpainted planks, the roof sod. There was a corral and a shed and what appeared to be a bunkhouse large enough to accommodate only four or five men. A few head of scrubby-looking cows, branded XX, drifted down to the tank by the creaking windmill. Gordon sat his saddle in the shelter of a cottonwood, studying the layout ahead.

He saw Adam Chaney come out of the house with what appeared to be a book under his arm. He yawned, stretched, looked around and went back inside. The door to the bunkhouse was open. If there was anyone inside, they gave no sign.

Gordon loosened his gun in its holster and rode across the clearing. Chaney must have heard him coming, for he came to the door again. He gave Gordon a sardonic smile.

"I see you're still alive," he said.

Gordon swung down, studying the parchment-like face of this man he knew so little about. "You missed me and hit the lamp last night."

"Oh, come now, Gordon, you should know better than to try and trick me into anything. I never fired a gun at you or your lamp."

92

"Then your hired man. Tom Union."

Chaney shook his head. "You know better than that. If Union had been that close you wouldn't be here to tell me about it. Come inside, Gordon."

"We'll talk out here. I didn't know until today that you hired Union after MacLane fired him."

"Put it this way, Gordon. Union wanted a roof over his head. He came here . . . and—"

"You butted into our game in town the other night. Mine and Union's game. You warned him off. Why?"

"To save your neck," Chaney said patiently.

"I wonder."

"After that little episode in town I told Union he was no longer welcome here. Not that he ever was, but there were certain pressures involved."

"What pressures?"

"I'd rather not say." Chaney looked Gordon up and down. "Your return to this country has made certain people uneasy, Gordon."

"Yeah, I can imagine." His gaze held Chaney's.

"The fact that you've changed has— Well, you stood up to Union the other night. He's no fool. He was surprised that you didn't turn tail and run."

"Then he could have shot me in the back."

"Gordon, I've always liked you. I've been a dreamer too. I can sympathize with a man like you. And you *are* a man now. No longer a boy. Get out of this country. There is nothing for you here."

"There are things to be done."

"You mean vengeance." Chaney was thoughtful for a moment. "Don't do it, Gordon."

"That's what Opal said."

"I know that girl. I know her better than my sister Charlotte does. Or her Uncle Roland. If you came back because of Opal, take her away."

"I didn't come back for that."

Impatience touched Chaney's eyes. He stood aside. "I want to show you something."

Gordon hesitated, then entered Chaney's house. If you could call it a house. It was a two-room shack, with a cot and two chairs and a table. It had a two-burner wood stove. Against one wall were shelves of books.

Chaney pointed to the books. "Those are tools, Gordon. A gun is no tool. It's a destroyer. Leave the shooting to

93

men like Union."

"He killed my wife."

"So Opal told me. But nothing you can do will bring her back. Don't you see, there are certain people in this world who must lead. And they must do it by gentle means. Not with guns. There is a place for dreamers in this world."

"You're a dreamer, you said." Gordon looked significantly around the small quarters. "And this is all you got out of it?"

A faint flush touched Chaney's face. "It took me a long time to find myself. But time is on your side. You're young. I'm much older. Go away, Gordon. Get yourself an education. Read books—"

There was the sound of horses approaching. A quick fear touched Gordon and Chaney said, "Don't worry, it isn't Union. He won't come back here."

Through the window Gordon could see Rin Orland riding up. With the 77 foreman were the three men who had been at his side the day Gordon and Blackhorn had come back to this country.

"Conners," Orland called as he neared the house. "I want to talk to you."

Gordon hesitated, then stepped out. Orland drew up, his three men spreading out a little. Orland pushed back his blanket coat with his elbows. The black-handled gun loomed darkly at his belt. "I've got something to say, Conners."

"How'd you know I was here?"

"We saw you riding this way." Orland drew his black-butted gun so swiftly Gordon was stunned with surprise. Orland cocked the weapon, nodded at the rider on his left. "All right, Al."

Al shook out his saddle rope. Chaney, standing at Gordon's elbow said, "Now wait a minute, Orland—"

"Keep out of this, Chaney," Orland said coldly. "He won't get hurt—much."

Gordon tried to dodge the loop that sailed for his head. He turned, grabbing for his gun, but the noose clamped down. Al drew back. Gordon was thrown heavily. Dazed, he tried to get up but two of Orland's men jumped him. One knocked him back with a looping blow to the side of his head. The rope was slipped down under Gordon's armpits, drawn tight. The second man unbuckled Gordon's gun rig.

And during this time Gordon was being slowly dragged across the uneven ground.

"Not too fast, Al," Orland cautioned, and the rider moved his horse at a walk across the yard. The horse picked up speed gradually, and Gordon tried to get free of the rope. But he had no success.

"You'll kill him!" Chaney shouted.

"Just keep out of it," Orland warned.

Gordon didn't remember much else. His body bumped across the yard. He choked on dust. A rock jutting from the ground scraped his forehead. He felt the burning of his skin as the earth slid under him. Later he began to scream. He felt his shirt go and then his britches as he was dragged through a thicket.

The sun clouded over and it was very dark.

When he opened his eyes he saw Rin Orland's dark face above him. "This is your warning, Conners. I work for a big outfit. The owners don't like losses. You're a suspected rustler. This is my way of telling you to clear out. I can't take a chance on a known rustler. Next time I'll rope your neck to a tree."

The men rode off. Adam Chaney helped him to the house. Gordon lay on a cot in his tattered underwear. He felt as if every inch of skin had been burned off his body.

He saw Chaney filling kettles, putting them on the wood stove. Chaney dragged out a tin tub. He saw that Gordon's eyes were open. He got a bottle of whisky. He forced a drink down Gordon's throat. Gordon gagged. The second drink he kept down.

"There was a time," Chaney said, "when they burned the dreamers at the stake. Now they drag them at the end of a rope."

"But why—why?"

Chaney gave him a long bitter look. He took a drink out of the bottle, corked it. "Could it be said any plainer, Gordon? You're not safe here. If you stay, they'll kill you."

"But—"

"Listen to me. Anvil is a big outfit. Bigger than Seventy-Seven. The biggest in this end of the country. The owners live in England. They've been hard hit by the rustling. They're going broke. Somebody is going to be able to buy Anvil for ten cents on the dollar. That somebody is not going to let you stand in his way."

"I won't run. My pa ran all his life. I—won't run!"

"You're mule-headed. For God's sake, listen—"

The first of the kettles on the stove began to give off steam. Chaney filled the tin tub. The soap was homemade, wood ashes and pork fat. It made a thick yellow suds and burned like turpentine in Gordon's cuts. He was glad to see that he had not been as skinned up as he supposed. But his injuries were bad enough.

Through the steam rising around him he could see some of the names on the books on the shelf, Confucius, Lao-tze, Plato, Voltaire—

"You talk about books, education," Gordon said bitterly. "All the books in the world couldn't keep Orland from draggin' me."

"Remember, he let you off fairly easy. He could have killed you."

"Only a gun would keep him off me an' you were too yellow to use one on him."

"I'm not a gunfighter," Chaney said, flushing.

Gordon glanced around at the books again. "What were you before you came here? A professor or something?"

"I never finished school," Chaney said. He looked down at the old callouses on his hands. "My mother and father died of the cholera when I was thirteen. I went to work in the Kentucky coal mines to keep Charlotte and myself alive. She married soon after. I guess that's the only escape, for a girl. I lost touch with her. I was sick of the mines . . . started trying to educate myself. I don't like to remember what it took. Going without food to buy books, trying to study after fourteen hours of shoveling coal, so exhausted I couldn't think, sick most of the time, never warm enough. I—became a bookkeeper for a big cattle outfit in Dakota. I saved my money. My sister learned where I was and asked me to come here. This place was for sale. I bought it."

Gordon looked up through the clouds of steam at Chaney, trying to see any resemblance between this man and Charlotte Bayard. "You just don't seem like Charlotte's brother."

"Roland has indulged her," Chaney said. "Spoiled her. She's like a greedy kid, never able to get enough to eat. I guess you can't blame her. Seeing how they live, it's hard to remember the winters we went without shoes, the nights she cried herself to sleep because I hadn't brought home any food. She wants me to come and live with them. She thinks I'm crazy. I'm interested in helping the Chinese in Ricetown. They were brought here by the railroad years ago. Now they're charged exorbitant rents for those shacks. The Chinese have given me friendship. I feel as if I'm doing something worthwhile in trying to help them."

Gordon looked surprised. "The railroad owns the shacks in Ricetown. So that puts you on the opposite side of the fence from your brother-in-law. You'll fight him to help the Chinese?"

"Roland is involved, yes," Chaney said. "The owner of that property is making a fortune out of rentals to the Chinese—"

"You mean the railroad?"

"The railroad doesn't—" Chaney broke off. "The same as the owners of Seventy-Seven are going to make a fortune in beef this year."

Gordon climbed stiffly out of the tub, dripping water. He dried himself with a towel Chaney handed him. He looked down at the cuts on his body, the bruises turning purple. Yes, Orland could have had him dragged to death. Then he thought of something else.

"I don't remember much of what happened out there," Gordon said thinly. "Did Orland search me?"

"He went through your pockets, what was left of them."

"I figured he did." Gordon gave Chaney a long look. "I don't understand you, Adam. You talk in riddles. You warn me out and when I don't warn very good, Rin Orland comes along. He drags me at the end of a rope. And he warns me. Then you take me in and let me use your bathtub . . . and you talk about books and education. You talk about the Chinese in Ricetown and how they're bein' cheated. You talk about the money Seventy-Seven is goin' to make in beef. It's all tied together someway, isn't it?"

"The world is tied together, Gordon. We're all brothers. You and I, the Chinese. The blackest African, the fairest Norseman. . . . Can't you see, Gordon? I like you. I'm trying to help. To show you, if I can. After years of search I found myself, after a fashion. You can find yourself. But not here. Not in Table Rock."

Chaney had laid out a pair of linsey-woolsey pants and

a shirt bleached the color of chalk by countless washings in wheat settlings. Gordon's own clothes had been torn to pieces in the yard.

Chaney said, "Opal told me about the holdup note."

Gordon looked at him quickly. "She did?"

"It's obviously what Rin Orland was after." Chaney cleared his throat. "I presume you have it hidden in a safe place."

"Yeah."

"You know, Gordon, that note can help no one now. It can't bring back the dead, your father, your mother. Burn the note, Gordon."

Gordon shook his head.

"Then give it to someone for safe keeping," Chaney urged.

"Roland Bayard had the same idea. He wanted to keep it for me."

"Why didn't you let him?"

"What good would that do? It doesn't really matter where the note is. When the time comes I'll match up somebody's handwritin' with it."

"That somebody may not wait. He may take a hot iron to the bottoms of your feet and make you tell where you hid it."

"Who, Adam? You?" Gordon limped to a small table by the bookshelf where his gun rig rested. He buckled on the gun.

Adam, watching him, said, "If I was the one after that note, I certainly wouldn't leave your gun where you could get it."

Gordon frowned. He examined the weapon to see that it hadn't been tampered with. "Thanks for what you done for me, Adam. I won't forget it."

Chapter Fifteen

IT WAS HARD to sit his saddle, because there was hardly an area of his body that had not been scraped or bruised. He had been dragged slowly at the end of a rope and he was in bad shape. What would have happened if Rin Orland had given the order to spur that horse. Gordon shuddered at the thought.

As he rode he flexed the fingers of his right hand. They were stiffening. The old fear came back with a rush. What gun speed would he have now? Would the fingers slow him if it came to the showdown with Union? All the way home he kept working the stiffness out of the fingers.

Blackhorn still was not at the dugout. Gordon ate some cold biscuits, reheated the coffee. He tried to think, to piece together the pieces of the puzzle that were lying in his brain like jagged shards of glass. Cutting him, nagging him. Maybe he was a fool. Maybe he really should get out. A sudden panic swept him, and he tried to fight it.

He went to the rock where he had left the wallet, and retrieved it. He stuck it in his belt and buttoned his shirt over it. Then he took a look at the sod house that had played such a part in his life. He turned his back on it and rode away. He would not come back. He would find Blackhorn and they would go deep into the mountains and forget everything that had happened. There was no use in asking for death and that was what would happen if Gordon stayed. Chaney had warned him, Rin Orland had warned him. The sheriff and MacLane also had made it plain he was unwelcome and risked his neck by staying.

He expected to find Blackhorn at the Caboose saloon, which the man had indicated was his favorite in Table Rock. Keeping to a back alley, his hat brim pulled low, Gordon entered town. He tethered Spades behind a hotel and moved through a slot between this structure and the bank. He glanced at the second floor windows where Bayard had his office. He thought of seeing Bayard, shaking his hand, thanking him for being a friend to his folks for so many years. But he didn't want to chance running into Opal there as he had the other day. His mind was made up and he didn't want anything to change it. Seeing Opal again might revive some foolish dreams.

He stood for a moment on the busy walk of the main street, studying the crowd. He saw no sign of Tom Union. Or anyone else he knew, for that matter. He worked the bruised right hand and was glad none of his fingers had been incapacitated during the business with Orland's men.

He angled across the street toward the Caboose.

"Gordon! Gordon Conners!"

It was a girl's voice. He turned, seeing Opal standing in

99

a shop doorway in the middle of the block. In her hand she held a pin cushion full of pins. A tape measure was looped over her arm.

Removing his hat, he walked to where she stood. A sign on a window said, Ladie's Shoppe.

She stared at his skinned, bruised face. "Gordon, what happened?"

"I fell down."

She showed disbelief. "I've taken that job, Gordon," she said. "I'm no longer living with Uncle Roland and Aunt Charlotte."

"I—I hope it's what you want."

"I'm boarding with Mrs. Anderson. She owns the shop. I—" She halted, embarrassed. "I'm sorry I acted like a silly girl at your place, Gordon. But I was so worried about you and—"

"You're not worried now?"

He saw the quick tears that came to her eyes. "You know better than that." She touched his arm. "Your coming to town today is sort of a—an omen. Uncle Roland is in his office. I just saw him go upstairs. Will you talk to him. Will you tell him everything and let him use his influence?"

"It wouldn't do any good."

"Yes it would. And when it's over I'm sure uncle could get you a job with the railroad—"

"Does Billy Halleck still come to the house? And the rest of them. Do they still court you?"

She shook her head. "I can't understand why I thought they were anything at all. A year later, they're still doing the same things. The saloon, cards, the latest devilment. So empty, Gordon, so aimless."

Her hair had always made him think of corn-tassel. He remembered the hungers he had known with Willa, the things he couldn't put into words. He felt a sudden sense of guilt again, of betraying Willa. Less than a year in her grave. And here he was feeling the same things in the presence of Opal that he had felt with Willa.

"I—I got to go," he said awkwardly.

"You won't talk with Uncle Roland?"

"I'm goin' away for a spell, and—"

She showed a mixture of relief and disappointment. Relief that he would be out of danger by leaving. Disappointment that they would be apart.

100

"Write to me, Gordon. Please let me know where you are. Please."

"I will," he promised, but he knew he never would. He would not ruin her life as he had Willa's. Knowing him had meant destruction for Willa. He couldn't do that to Opal. "I'll let you know," he said, and forced his stiffened lips into a smile.

He went down to the corner of the block and looked back. She was still watching him. She waved and he lifted his hand. He went around the side of the Caboose and entered by the rear door. Blackhorn was not inside. Gordon drank a bottle of beer, his eyes on the front door. He listened to talk of coal and cattle and railroad.

Worry deepened in him. He thought of the rustled horses MacLane and the buyer Tiny Ware had lost. Was Blackhorn's absence merely a coincidence? Maybe, but it had raised a nagging suspicion in Gordon's mind that he could not put aside. He remembered the man Blackhorn had been talking to in the saloon, on the day of their arrival. Thimblerig, Blackhorn had called him. And they had been talking about stock . . . the primest in the country!

He managed to get the barkeep's eye and ask his questions. The man didn't know Blackhorn. He did know Thimblerig by Gordon's description, but he couldn't tell Gordon where to find him.

Gordon, moving cautiously, tried another saloon, and another. Maybe Blackhorn was dead drunk by now, nursing his grudge in some side street hotel room. Gordon tried several of them, but found no trace of Blackhorn. The worry deepened.

He was heading back for his horse when he heard a familiar voice.

"Find the pea, gentlemen, the little goober under the thimble, only three thimbles and one pea, two-to-one, an idiot could figure that out, the odds are two-to-one, that you'll find it, any baboon from the island of Madagascar could add it up, how can you lose, I take no bets from bearded twins, one-legged grandmothers, or Igorotes with papers proving they are the illegitimate sons of Napoleon Bonapart. . . ."

It was Thimblerig, on the corner by the bank, standing behind his collapsible table. There were a few men watching him. The three thimbles were upturned on top of the table and he was moving them about before the eyes of the gaping onlookers. When he saw Gordon coming, he folded his table and tried to run. Gordon caught him, pinned him against the side wall of the bank. Those who had been watching, drifted away.

Gordon held Thimblerig by the lapels. The coat collar dug deep into the doughy folds of flesh.

"Why'd you try and get away?" Gordon demanded.

"Blackhorn said you'd likely try an' horn in on our deal—"

"Where is he?"

"I dunno—I dunno—"

"Yes you do," Gordon said. "What about this deal of yours? He's been gone too long—and you know where he is."

The man struggled and Gordon shook him till the collapsible table fell from his fat hand, spilling the thimbles on the sidewalk.

Thimblerig got his breath. "He's at Washakie Rocks. But leave him be. He don't want to see you!"

Gordon let him sag back against the building, staring at the sweating, fat-creased face. Washakie Rocks. Gordon knew it must be the truth. Thimblerig wouldn't know about it unless Blackhorn told him. The place was about five hours' ride to the north. It was where Blackhorn and Gordon had camped on the last night before reaching Table Rock.

Thimblerig was staring beyond Gordon. Alerted to possible danger, Gordon turned. He saw Roland Bayard standing at the door to the stairway that led to the railroad offices above the bank.

Thimblerig scampered away.

Bayard crossed to Gordon. "You won't find out anything about MacLane from a man like him," Bayard said, pointing at Thimblerig just disappearing around a corner of the bank building.

Gordon looked at him. "Do you know Thimblerig?"

"You forget how long I've worked for the railroad, Gordon. I know most of the con men who follow the tracks."

"Maybe I've quit tryin' to find out about MacLane," Gordon said.

Bayard looked blank, and Gordon told him what had

happened. Bayard bowed his head thoughtfully. His thick black hair, graying at the temples, smelled faintly of pomade. His jaws were smooth and flushed from a fresh shave and his nails were manicured. It made Gordon realize, curiously, what a different world from his own Opal had been brought up in.

Bayard said, "If it isn't MacLane, did you ever think what a will-o-the-wisp you're looking for? That holdup involving your father happened twenty years ago. So much could happen. The man who planned the holdup could be on the other side of the world now, or dead—"

"Tom Union was in on it. He ain't dead."

"Maybe he's the only one left. Maybe there isn't anybody else." Bayard stepped closer. "Gordon, listen to me. Union's name is mentioned in that note. It would still convict him of the holdup. I suggest you bring the note to me—you still have it of course—and then we'll have a talk with Sheriff Simms—"

"I got to do it my way." Gordon started away, then turned back. "Who owns Seventy-Seven?"

Bayard pursed his lips. "Some syndicate out of St. Louis, so I've heard. Why?"

"Did you know they figure to buy out that English-owned outfit, Anvil, for ten cents on the dollar?"

"Where did you hear such nonsense?"

"Adam Chaney told me."

With a forefinger Bayard thoughtfully touched one of his thick, graying sideburns. "My brother-in-law, it seems, has a vivid imagination."

"Did you know that Tom Union is now workin' at Seventy-Seven?"

"Well, yes. As a matter of fact I did hear that. Just today."

Bayard had been staring curiously at Gordon's bruises. He asked what had happened to him. Gordon told him.

"Rin Orland ordered you dragged at the end of a rope?" He sounded incredulous. "I don't understand it. I just don't understand it."

"Neither do I," Gordon said.

Bayard removed a watch from his vest pocket, glanced at it and then said he had an appointment in another part of town. He hurried away.

Gordon rode Spades out of town, in the direction of

Washakie Rocks. He wondered if ever again in his life-time he would set foot in Table Rock. When he thought of Opal he felt a sadness he could not suppress.

Chapter Sixteen

As THE HOURS PASSED the stiffness in Gordon's body seemed intensified. But he kept working his right hand so that his fingers would remain pliant. It was a long ride to Washakie Rocks. He followed the road. During the winter the snow drifted so deep that tall willows had been planted along the road to mark the route. The dark clay banks were streaked with white shale and the distant mountains were touched by the sun. Greasewood flats filled the wind with a tar-and-turpentine smell and somewhere deep in the alkali desert a coyote began howl-ing.

When it turned dark he felt his hunger. He found some jerky in his saddlebags. He spent the night on the flats and started again before dawn. Just at first light he reached the badlands where the desert had been scoured into a labyrinth by wind and water. The Rocks were a tumbled heap of sandstone pillars well off the road. They would have been lost in the maze of gullies and gorges, unless a man knew the landmarks.

Gordon remembered the turnoff they had taken when they had camped here before. He turned into one of the miniature gorges. In a moment the road was lost be-hind. Gordon followed the twisting gorge till it was bro-ken by a transverse gulch. If the gulch had been deeper it would have been a box canyon. Across its mouth a crude willow fence had been raised. A dusty bunch of horses were stirring sleepily near the dead-end.

Just outside the fenced mouth of the gulch was Black-horn's camp. His calico mule was tethered near a heap of camp gear and the old man was still rolled up in his blan-kets.

The mule heard Gordon's horse, or smelled it, and let out a bray. Blackhorn sat up. The old Joslyn-Tomes must have been under the blankets with him because the rifle was in his hands as soon as he was upright. Gordon rode within five feet and dismounted, glaring at the old man.

He crossed to the fire and saw a blackened running iron lying in the ashes.

"You're gettin' almighty careless," Gordon said. "If I was MacLane I could string you up right here."

Blackhorn wiped a hand across his greasy beard. Beside the blankets was an empty whiskey bottle. He picked up the bottle, saw there was no liquor left, and threw it across the clearing where it crashed against the rocks. The shattering glass spooked the horses beyond the enclosure.

"What's MacLane got to do with it?" Blackhorn said, without looking at him.

"Quit makin' smoke. Those are Crazy Moon horses in that pen. How could you pull such a damnfool stunt? They killed my pa for this very thing."

Blackhorn rose stiffly, scratched himself. "Your pa was an amateur. Nobody's agoin' to ketch Blackhorn."

"Is this your way of gettin' back at me? Doin' some crazy thing like this so I'll fret an' worry."

"You don't give a hang what happens to ol' Blackhorn." He reeked of whiskey, both his breath and his ragged clothes.

"You been a friend to me, Blackhorn. Course I worry." Gordon clapped a hand on a bony shoulder. "You're mad on account I talked sweet about Opal. Forget it. I'm not goin' back. You an' me are goin' back to Wind Rivers."

"What about Tom Union?"

"Someday, somewhere he'll git what's comin' to him. All of a sudden I got the feelin' it ain't up to us to settle him."

"You'd run out," Blackhorn accused.

"You ran out."

Blackhorn fingered his nose. "Yeah, reckon I did. A man gits his belly fulla forty-rod an' his brain don't work no more."

"It was a loco stunt stealin' these hosses."

"Reckon. But Thimblerig told me about this deal . . . slick as a greased pig . . . a buyer travelin' through from Cheyenne. He'll pick up these hosses today and have 'em in Idaho by tomorrow."

Gordon limped twenty feet to the fence. The light was growing stronger and he could see that the brand on the horses was a big Teacup. It was a clever way to change the Crazy Moon and in Idaho nobody would question. "I got to hand it to you," Gordon said. "You're good. Damned good."

"I told you I was the greatest hoss thief in the world. A man's got to keep his hand in or he loses his touch."

"Light the fire, Blackhorn. You're changin' these brands back to Crazy Moon."

"Jigger, don't be crazy. I can't do that. There's enough money there to make us comfortable the rest o' the year. No sod house, no gittin' lean in the belly, no—"

Gordon came back and in the growing daylight in the canyon Blackhorn apparently got his first good look at his face. Gordon turned his back.

"What in hell happened to you?" Blackhorn demanded.

Gordon told him. Blackhorn looked grim. "So Tom Union's workin' for Seventy-Seven. Mebby you're right, son. Mebby we better clear out. An' we won't stop to change no brands—"

Gordon's back was still turned when Blackhorn broke off. Gordon heard a shuffling sound, and then Blackhorn's shout.

"Jigger—"

There was the deafening crash of a shot. Gordon wheeled to see Blackhorn down on one knee, the Joslyn-Tomes in his hands. He had taken the shot at the dim shape of a horseman on the edge of the gully above them. The man's horse shied and the rider, who had been trying to aim a rifle, made a loose sidelong fall out of the saddle. He came bouncing down the sandstone slope, arms flopping. He landed not ten feet away. Gordon felt a sudden churning sickness. Blackhorn's shot had torn away part of the man's face.

There was a shot, then another. Blackhorn was yelling for Gordon to seek cover. And the old man's voice brought Gordon out of his sickness. He spun, drawing his gun. He could see riders charging along the wash now, five of them, their horses raising great gouts of dust. And in the lead he saw the big man with the hard hat. Tom Union. Union's gun spat at Gordon. Gordon heard the lethal sucking breath of the projectile past his ear. Without stopping to consider his move at all Gordon dropped the hammer. But Union's horse took the bullet. Blackhorn finished the job. Rider and horse came down in a squealing plunge. The rider behind Union tried to draw rein. The racing mount's shoulder scraped the rump of the falling horse.

In the thick cloud of dust Gordon saw this second rider unseated, saw him scamper to his feet, swing back into the saddle of his horse that had recovered from the near fall. Union's horse was thrashing on the ground. Union lay some distance away, face down on the hard ground. His hat was a dozen yards nearer the gate of the makeshift corral. The penned horses were plunging, making shrill sounds of fear.

Blackhorn's rifle cracked and a rider sagged and dropped his gun. Blood spurted from the tips of his fingers. He rode back the way he had come, leaning over in the saddle. The horse that had stumbled into Union's mount was limping badly. Its rider cut out of the canyon as fast as his injured mount could carry him. The other two riders, evidently having enough, wheeled and went after him. One of them twisted around in the saddle and fired. Blackhorn, a little behind Gordon and to one side, gave a grunt and sat down heavily.

In a rage Gordon emptied his gun at the man who had fired. The man fell and his riderless horse plunged on after the remaining three horsemen. Gordon rushed to Blackhorn. But Blackhorn coughed, tried to say something, then fell back.

Gordon had an urge to ride after the survivors. But he held back. Instead of the thunder of guns frightening him it only served to crystallize his anger. He knew if he trailed the riders they'd see him coming and 'bush him in some canyon. Sick, he looked down at Blackhorn. The old man was dead.

Gordon stared numbly at Blackhorn. The horses in the corral had quieted. Union's horse no longer thrashed. Union was beginning to moan. Flies had already started to mat the shattered face of the dead man beyond. Fifty yards up the canyon the other man lay unmoving.

As Gordon looked again at Blackhorn he remembered the numbness when he had knelt beside his dead father and mother at the sod house. He remembered how he had thought there was something wrong with him because he couldn't feel anything. And how it had come later, the way the agony of a bad wound came later, after the shock wore off. There had been times when he hated Blackhorn. There were other times when he had felt closer to the old man than to his own father.

Gordon felt himself shaking. He didn't know how long he had been doing it. He knew it hadn't come at first. It had all happened too fast, the way it had when he'd shot the bear, with no time for panic. But he could feel no triumph. It was coming now. He could hear the echoes of the shots, in his head. He knew they had long since died, but he could still hear them. His hands were clammy, and it was hard to breathe. But he forced himself to breathe deeply, and soon the spasm passed. He reloaded his gun.

Union flopped over on his side. Gordon saw then that the man had been shot low. Union was holding his belly with both hands where Blackhorn's bullet had taken him. Gordon crossed over, looked down at him.

"You killed my wife," he said hoarsely.

Union's shirt, just above the belt buckle, was soaked with blood. The stain also appeared through Union's spread fingers, and was on the backs of his hands. The hard hat lay in the dust a dozen feet away.

"A drink," Union gasped. The effort of speaking twisted his face with pain.

Gordon backed up to where Blackhorn's canteen lay. He brought it over and knelt beside Union and the man sucked greedily on it.

"How'd you know I was here, Union? Who was with you?"

"Some of the Seventy-Seven boys," Union said. He fell back and the canteen tipped, spilling out some of the water. Gordon replaced the cork.

"Who was in it with you? Your partner in the holdup, I mean. Is it Rin Orland?"

Union's face was getting gray. "Orland ain't much older than you. The holdup was twenty years ago."

"Yeah. I never thought of that." Gordon was watching the canyon ahead, scanning the ridges. The three riders might return. But one of them was wounded. That left two. They might chance jumping him, or they might ride for help.

"And I thought it was MacLane in it with you," Gordon said bitterly. He was thinking that this man Union was getting off too easy. He had wanted to face Union and draw his gun and beat him. And then as Union lay dying, tell him about Willa. Union was dying all right, but it was Blackhorn who'd done it. Maybe it was better this way, Gordon thought. Blackhorn avenging his daughter. It was the last thing the old man had done in this life.

"MacLane. . . ." Union started to laugh. A cough convulsed him and blood foamed into his mustaches. It was a long time before he could stop coughing. "No, it sure wasn't MacLane," he said at last.

"Then who?"

"He was always the smart one," Union said. His eyes were glazing. "The way he figured out that holdup—a body could've known how it would be. I shoulda been smart too. Had to show off . . . blew my share in six months . . . women, poker, buck the tiger . . . My poke gettin' littler all the time while his was gettin' bigger . . . brains, politics, investments . . . one step after the other, right up the ladder, damn cat with his damn cream—"

Union was talking in breathless gusts, making random motions with one bloody hand, so far gone he didn't seem aware of Gordon any more. "He thought I come back to crawl, didn't he? Well, I didn't. I come back . . . get what's due me. He had to pay, believe me . . . what I know . . . He couldn't let me talk. He'll pay even bigger for this." His gaze shifted. "The note he wrote. You got it, Conners. We'll take it to him an' he'll pay us both . . . pay us big . . ."

He began coughing blood again. Gordon grabbed his arm.

"Who, Union—who? Only two men knew I was heading here. You aren't talking about Thimblerig. Is it Bayard? He overheard me an' Thimblerig talkin'. Is it Roland Bayard?"

Union had pressed his bloodied right hand inside his shirt as if to ease his pain. And now the hand came out holding a derringer. Gordon reacted instinctively, flinging himself aside. He heard the roar of the weapon. On hands and knees he drew his Colt as Union, his lips taut with pain, swung the gun for its second shot.

Gordon fired and saw the bullet strike a point just above the bridge of Union's nose. Union fell back. He didn't move.

"We got him for you, Willa," Gordon said in a voice husky with emotion. "Me an' Blackhorn got him."

He looked down at the derringer Union had dropped. The brush with death had not brought even a quiver to Gordon's nerves. He wondered then if the pendulum had swung too far the other way. Today he had killed and he felt no remorse. His hand was not shaking. He reloaded his gun.

He turned, intending to scoop out a grave for Black-horn but the ground began to shake. He straightened slowly, cocking his head to listen. In the far distance there was a thunder of hoofbeats.

Chapter Seventeen

QUICKLY GORDON RUSHED down the wash where Spades had drifted against the gate in the willow fence Blackhorn had built across the mouth of the gulch. He swung into the saddle and lifted the rawhide loop that held the gate closed. The pressure of the horses behind the gate swung it open. The rustled horses rushed out and along the wash. Gordon sent Spades climbing a steep slant that led to the top of a sandstone bluff. Here he had a good view of the surrounding countryside. Coming at a dead run from the east was a large body of riders. Not more than a quarter of a mile away. Those in the lead had seen him silhouetted on the bluff. There were a scattering of shots. The riders veered in his direction.

Gordon looked toward the north, wondering if he could find sanctuary in that direction. But the country was rougher than it was to the south and the riders were swinging in a wide arc from that direction. They'd cut him off in any one of fifty blind canyons. He spurred his horse and sent it rocketing downslope, angling for the stage road in the distance.

In the hills he was out of sight of the riders, but they were still coming. Glancing back occasionally he could see their dust. Why wasn't the day ending instead of just beginning? he groaned. Darkness would hide him. But now, in broad daylight . . . He felt a hard core of fear lodge in his throat. Not a fear of guns, but a fear of what would happen if they caught him. He was remembering what Sheriff Simms had said about there being worse things than death by gunfire in a sod house.

As he rode he thought of what the dying Tom Union had said. Roland Bayard was the only one who fitted the description of the man Union talked about. Brains, politics, investments, one step after the other. And twenty years ago, how did Bayard fit? Whoever planned the hold-up had to be in a trusted position. That had been obvious from the beginning. Somebody on the inside, knowing the schedule of the pay train, able to obtain false credentials, to get Bob Conners and Blackhorn aboard. And Roland Bayard had been a dispatcher at Julesburg, twenty miles away from Hairpin Crossing. He would have known the schedules. He could have gotten to the holdup at Hairpin Crossing while he was off-shift, and could have returned to Julesburg with nobody the wiser. Gordon remembered how Bayard had offered to keep the holdup note in his safe. All the little pieces, one by one, falling into place.

He switched his trail a dozen times, heading west, then doubling back. Once he tried swinging toward the north, but they were ahead of him, trying to search out his trail in the badlands they were crossing. He moved away quickly and hoped they hadn't seen him. Spades was tiring and Gordon knew he would have to get another horse if the pursuit continued, and he saw no reason why it shouldn't.

Gordon would have to steal a fresh mount. He would be a horse thief just like Blackhorn.

And suddenly, just thinking of the old man, released the grief he had been holding back. Gordon didn't know much about praying. He'd never been inside a church in his life, but his mother had read Scripture to him when he was little. He tried to remember some of it now, but it was all beyond him.

He halted, looked back. There was no longer any dust. Maybe he had eluded them, but only for the time being.

Dusk came finally and he halted by a creek. He and the horse drank. There was grass for Spades, but no food for Gordon. He pulled in his belt. Far in the distance now he could see the lights of Table Rock. There in that town was Roland Bayard. He didn't want to believe it about Bayard. The man had been his father's best friend. Bayard had taken Gordon and his mother in after the holdup. Yet that could have been an attempt to get the holdup note. If that note matched Bayard's handwriting Bayard was damned. He had climbed so high, he stood to lose so much.

Gordon made a decision. Before he left this country he wanted to know the truth. If Bayard was guilty he must pay. . . .

But could he get to town without being seen? He considered his position. He hoped his pursuers would feel it unlikely that he would risk going back to town. Maybe they would continue looking for him in the hill country. Of course, come daylight, his tracks would be picked up again, for they were out of the badlands now.

It was seven o'clock by the time Gordon reached Table Rock. He sat the saddle of his jaded horse, seeing no light in Bayard's office above the bank. He rode on to the Bayard house, two miles from town. The perfumed smell of the poplar grove in front of the long gallery reminded him of that night so long ago when he had sought safety here. He remembered how Bayard had asked him about the note that night, the insistent question, "Did your father give you anything?" He remembered how Opal's reappearance with the food had kept Bayard from questioning him further.

There were no horses around the house. Lamplight glowed at the windows. He thought of the times he had seen Opal through those windows when he rode past. Or seen some of her suitors on the porch, and once she had called to him as he passed, and he pretended not to hear. He remembered hearing Billy Halleck's derisive laughter that night.

Gordon left Spades at the south side of the house. Quietly he climbed the porch steps. His right ankle pained him and he limped. He must have turned it again when he twisted aside to avoid the lethal shot from Union's derringer. He had a bruise on his left knee and a rock cut on his thigh. His ribs were sore to the touch. Rin Orland's man had done a good job.

He wondered who had been after him today. More 77 men probably. The trio fleeing from the fight in the gulch had more than likely run into a bunch of 77 riders out on the range.

Gordon tried the panelled front door. It was unlocked. Without knocking he slipped into the house.

Charlotte Bayard, seated on a stuffed Cordovan ottoman in the center of the room, was tugging peevishly at a thread caught in the inevitable needlework. She looked up in surprise.

"Ah—Gordon." She seemed a little frightened. "You—you startled me. Roland said you were back. We—we intended having you out for supper some night. What happened to your face? Come in, come in. Careful to your left—that's my new bust. Carrara marble, all the way from Europe."

Gordon was so tired he could hardly stand. "Where's Roland?"

His harsh voice caused her to lift her gaze from the tangled needlework. "You've changed, Gordon. You sound almost—belligerent."

"Where is he, Charlotte?"

"He's not in. Do you think the bust will go with our new motif? The Veiled Vestal, they call it. I'm having the whole room done over in marble. I'm so tired of this flock paper—"

"I want Roland," Gordon said. Empty-headed female, he thought. How could Bayard have stood her all these years? She was still a handsome woman and had her figure, corseted as it might be. But the endless chatter, the decorating, the redecorating of her home would drive a man insane.

"Roland went to bring Opal back, of course. Silly child . . . Did she think we'd let her work? The niece of Roland Bayard? I should say not. She'll be over her pique—Gordon, if you'd like to wait you can examine my Boulton ware. It's salt-glazed pottery, you know, and so hard to ship without breaking." She barely paused for breath, "Cook's gone to town but will return shortly. Adam is coming for supper tonight. Why don't you join us—"

Gordon looked around the big room. His eyes were bitter. A man had died today. His friend Blackhorn. And this woman with her vanity, her senseless, wandering thoughts. "It must cost a lot of money to keep a woman like you happy," he said.

"I know nothing of money." She giggled. "Roland never shows me the bills."

"Is that why he did it?"

"Did it? I don't understand you, Gordon."

"He couldn't give you all this fancy stuff. Not on a dispatcher's salary, could he?"

She was at the mantel, taking down a piece of the Boulton ware. "He had investments. He was always shrewd with his money."

"If you've got a good size chunk of money to start with it helps. A man can be mighty shrewd when he's got it buried in the back yard."

Charlotte gave him a blank look. She put the piece of Boulton ware back on the mantel.

"Does Roland keep any of his business papers here?" Gordon asked.

She turned, frowning prettily. "Business papers?"

He crossed to her, shaking her. "Charlotte, you got to live in this world. You ain't in it at all. You're in a world of your own. With this—" he flung out a hand to encompass the room— "this junk."

"Young man, do you realize—"

Gordon spotted a piece of paper lying on a cherrywood table. He crossed over.

Charlotte, dearest:
I think we've given Opal enough time to come back on her own and apologize. I've gone into town to bring her back. I'm sure she'll have a different attitude now. A day in that shop will prove to her that we can provide a much better life.
                              Your devoted, Roland.

Gordon didn't have to take out the wallet with the other note. He knew without comparing them. But he did it anyway, laying the two pieces of paper side by side, unwilling to accept what he saw. The writing didn't match.

Charlotte had folded daintily into a nearby chair, rustling like an expiring sparrow. "Gordon . . . my smelling salts—I can't understand you . . . if you're going to act this way I'll have to ask you not to come again."

Gordon returned the holdup note to his wallet. He stood slowly shaking his head from side to side, unable to believe what his eyes said was truth. Roland Bayard was not the man.

Chapter Eighteen

THERE WAS THE sound of a rig out front. Gordon stepped quickly to the front window, pulled aside a drape and peered out into the darkness. He saw Roland Bayard's handsome panel boot landau. Bayard, just alighting, stared at the house.

Gordon passed the wailing Charlotte, and went out to the gallery. He closed the door behind him. "Roland, I—"

Bayard looked up. "What are you doing here, Gordon?"

"Hear me out, Roland. Ten minutes ago if I'd seen you likely I'd have pulled a gun. But now—"

"You don't make sense, Gordon." Bayard had one foot on the gallery steps.

"Making sense is somethin' I'm not very good at to-night," Gordon admitted. "I thought you was the guilty man. The one who double-crossed my pa. I was wrong."

"Wrong—wrong?" Bayard's lips worked but there was no sound for a moment. Then he said, "I'm glad you've seen the light, Gordon. I had no idea you suspected me." Bayard looked back in the direction of town. He faced around. In the light spilling from the front windows his face was grim. "Gordon, you've got to get out of here. I was having my evening drink at the Caboose when Mac-Lane and his men rode in. They say you rustled some Crazy Moon horses—"

"I didn't, Roland. I swear it."

"Some of the Seventy-Seven boys found you first at a rustler camp. Gordon, MacLane is going to hang you. You've got to get away."

"But I didn't do it, Roland—"

"Listen to me closely. MacLane says that he and some of his men were hunting for the stolen horses. Some of the Seventy-Seven riders caught up with them. They said there'd been a fight in the badlands. They led them back to your camp. MacLane found Tom Union dead. Now I don't shed tears for a man like that. It's a relief to have him dead. But there were two other Seventy-Seven men killed, and one wounded. Hurry, Gordon. If there's ever anything I can do, just write me—"

"I—I don't know—"

Bayard held out his hand and Gordon went down the steps and took it and Bayard said, "Gordon, where can you go? Where can you hide?"

"I'm goin' to head south. I'll get to Mexico. I'll write you, Roland."

Bayard's fingers suddenly closed hard over Gordon's hand that he was clasping. "All right, Billy!" Bayard cried in a shrill, frightened voice.

115

Gordon tried to spin away as he heard a step behind him on the gallery. He caught a glimpse of Halleck, realized the man had ridden out from town with Bayard, had sneaked through the house and come up behind Gordon. They had evidently seen Gordon through one of the windows as they approached the house.

Desperately Gordon tried to free himself of Bayard's grip and at the same time reach for his gun with his left hand. But Halleck's revolver was out. Halleck came down the gallery steps, striking hard with the barrel of his gun.

Gordon was aware of pain and explosion inside his skull. He fell face down into one of Charlotte's freshly-spaded flower beds beside the gallery.

Bayard sounded agitated. "Billy, get to town. Tell Mac-Lane that Gordon is here."

"Shoot him now. You got every right to."

"No. I want MacLane to have the blame. Then Opal can't accuse me— Hurry, Billy. . . . Yes, I can handle him."

Gordon tried to get his eyes open. It felt as if someone had kindled a small fire at the back of his skull.

He heard Billy Halleck drive off in the landau.

Bayard said, "Charlotte, get back in the house! Do what I tell you!"

The front door closed.

There was silence.

Gordon managed to turn on his side. Dazedly he tried to paw dirt out of his eyes. Bayard loomed above him, holding a revolver. The hammer was back.

"Don't make me do it, Gordon," Bayard said tensely.

Gordon said, "My eyes, Roland—you got a handkerchief? A bandanna? I can't see—"

"I'm hardly fool enough to fall for a trick."

"It ain't no trick. I— Dirt in my eyes is killin' me."

Bayard gave a sound of exasperation. "Very well—" He leaned over, a white silk handkerchief dangling from the fingers of his left hand. Gordon caught the wrist, threw his weight on it. Bayard came plunging down into the flower bed beside him. The revolver discharged a shell into the ground. From the house sounded Charlotte's screams.

"You bastard you," Gordon cried and twisted the revolver out of Bayard's fingers. "You murderin' bastard!"

"Gordon, listen, please— Think of Opal. She loves you. She told me—I'm her uncle. Her blood relative—"

Gordon was pressing the muzzle of the revolver against Bayard's skull. Charlotte continued to scream inside the house.

"Tell me, goddamit, tell me!" Gordon said tensely. "I want to hear it all."

"All right." Bayard was gasping for breath. His eyes were wide with shock. There was dirt in his graying, well-kept hair. "I tricked your father. Yes, I wrote the note. I— But I did it for Charlotte. I—I never thought your father or Blackhorn would live to be taken prisoner. But they were and— I tried to make up for it to your father. I gave him money—"

"You tried to get your hands on that note. That was the only reason you was friends with us."

"I admit that, Gordon." He shifted his gaze, staring fearfully at the revolver Gordon held against his head. "Easy, boy. Easy. That gun has a hair trigger."

"I want the rest of it, Bayard!"

"I was paying Tom Union. Blackmail. I got him to rustle MacLane's cows and put them at your father's place. I couldn't afford scandal. You must understand that I am a man of influence in this community. People look up to me. I hold a responsible position with the railroad. And my wife— I love Charlotte, Gordon. Don't kill me, Gordon. You'll regret it all of your life."

"Will I?"

"Listen, boy." Sweat made Bayard's face slick as rain-swept window glass. "I can make it up to you. I can pay. I—I'll make you my representative at Seventy-Seven. Your father once told me how you always wanted to be in the cattle business like your uncle in Texas and—"

Gordon drew back, staring at the man groveling in the dirt beside him. Charlotte's screams had stopped. He supposed she had fainted.

"You and Seventy-Seven," Gordon said. "You own it."

"Yes, Gordon. You can have a job for the rest of your life. You and Opal get married. I—I'll give you a share of the profits, boy. Think of that. A quarter interest in Seventy-Seven. How does that strike you? And you can have a percentage of the rents I collect from the Chinese in Ricetown. I own that too, Gordon. I bought the land twenty years ago from the railroad. You'll have your future made, boy. Consider carefully."

"What happens when you an' that foreman of yours, Rin Orland, make Anvil go busted. You'll give me a share of that too, huh?"

Bayard gave a shaky laugh. "You're a hard bargainer, boy. Yes, anything I have is yours."

"It's Seventy-Seven doin' the wide-loopin'."

"Yes, I admit it. Rustling is a quick way to riches in the beef business—"

"Then those dead men were rustlers." Gordon's lips twisted. "The ones killed at Blackhorn's camp today."

"Boy, listen—"

"Along with everything else you're a lowdown thief!"

Suddenly Bayard tried to grab the gun out of Gordon's hand. Gordon hit him in the face with his left. Bayard whimpered. His eyes were glassy from shock. A trickle of blood moved from a corner of his mouth where Gordon's knuckles had struck.

"MacLane will be here!" Bayard cried. "He'll hang you!"

"You won't be here to see it, maybe."

"You can't kill me. It would be on your conscience. Opal would never forgive you."

"How much conscience does a dead man have?" Gordon got shakily to his feet. The back of his head ached. "You say MacLane will hang me? What difference does it make then whether I kill you or not?" He pointed the gun at the prostrate Bayard.

"My God, Gordon. You couldn't. Not in cold blood!"

"Who else is in on it? Why did Tom Union stay a spell with your brother-in-law? Did you force Adam to take him in?"

"Yes—yes. Forced isn't the word. I suggested Adam let him stay for a time, then got rid of him. I told Orland to give Union a job at Seventy-Seven—" Bayard broke off and some of the sick look had gone from his eyes. "Gordon, I took a shot at you out at your place. I shattered your lamp. I could have killed you. But I only wanted to frighten you. I hoped you'd leave and I wouldn't be forced to have you killed. I didn't want Opal—"

"Don't seem possible she's kin to a snake like you."

"You're not going to pull that trigger, Gordon," Bayard said, confidence once more restored to his voice. "You couldn't. You're not that kind."

"I'll only kill you if you try to get away."

For an instant Bayard looked relieved, then doubt touched his eyes. "What are you going to do with me?"

"I'm taking you to town. You tell your story to the sheriff."

A shrewdness was in the eyes now. "Of course, Gordon. I'll do whatever you say. After all, my boy, you have the upper hand."

Gordon studied the face of this man he had known for so long. The man his pa had trusted. "I guess town wouldn't be so good. I'll have to think of something else."

The brief hope died in Bayard's eyes.

"Maybe I'll let you tell MacLane when he gets here!"

"MacLane!"

"Tell him how you ordered Union to rustle Crazy Moon cows an' plant 'em at my pa's place. You killed my folks just as sure as if you'd pulled the trigger."

"MacLane wouldn't believe you!"

"You'll tell him. You'll make him a believer, Roland. I'm goin' to have your gun in your back. I'll kill you sure as hell's door has hinges."

He hauled Bayard to his feet.

There was a distant gunshot. Then another.

"They're coming," Bayard said hoarsely. "Get out, Gordon. Forget this crazy plan. Consider yourself fortunate to escape with your life."

Chapter Nineteen

GORDON WAS PEERING in the direction of town, listening for the first rumble of hoofbeats that would tell him Mac-Lane and his men were riding this way—with a rope. He thought he saw a flare of light toward town, but couldn't be sure. Maybe some of the riders would be carrying torches. This would be a spectacle—the hanging of Gordon Conners. Despite his holding a gun on Bayard he felt a chill. Bayard was also facing town, his hair and clothing flaked with damp earth from the flower bed.

There was a sound behind Gordon and he spun, the revolver swinging around. And on the gallery he saw Charlotte. Her hair had come unpinned and hung down on either side of her pale face. In her hands she held a double barreled shotgun. It was pointed at both of them.

Bayard also heard the sounds made by his wife coming to the gallery. For a moment he stood as if transfixed. Then, his voice a croak, he cried, "Charlotte, for God's sake watch it. You'll cut me to ribbons with that thing!"

Gordon knew he could drop the hammer of the revolver and it might speed a bullet into her body before she could react and send a screaming charge of buckshot into him. But he was frozen. It was one thing to face up to a man. He had killed Tom Union and felt no more remorse than when he'd cut down the grizzly with Blackhorn's rifle. But this—not a woman.

With a small cry Bayard broke clear, and Gordon tried to grab his coat sleeve. But Charlotte lifted the shotgun so that it covered Gordon alone.

"Keep away from him, Gordon!" she screamed.

Bayard, in the shadows by the corner of the house, said, "Keep him covered, Charlotte. Kill him if he moves."

"He's a destroyer!" Charlotte cried. "He wants to destroy my beautiful life. All the things I hold dear—"

"Charlotte," Gordon said. "Listen to me—"

Up on the gallery stood the woman with the shotgun. The hammers of the weapon were eared back. She kept biting her lips. Sweat moved across the powdered planes of her face, cutting small ugly paths.

"Drop it, Gordon," Bayard said. "The gun."

Gordon still clutched the revolver. His sweating hand refused to open and let the gun fall. The muscles of his chest were knotted against the anticipated smash of the buckshot.

"I'll count to five," Bayard said. "If he hasn't dropped that gun by then, Charlotte, cut him in two."

"Please go, Gordon," Charlotte wailed. "Please leave us alone. Go far away. I heard the terrible things you made Roland say."

"It's truth, Charlotte!" Gordon cried.

"No. Lies! Any man would lie when you hold a gun at his head and threaten to kill him!"

"Drop the gun, Gordon," Bayard said from a safe distance. "Charlotte's all worked up. All she has to do is touch one of those triggers and you're dead."

"I'll be dead anyhow. If you have your way."

"I'll give you a chance to run. I'll do that much for you, Gordon."

"And the minute I started to run you'd shoot me in the back," Gordon said bitterly.

Charlotte made a small hurt sound. "What a terrible thing to say, Gordon. Saying that to the man who befriended you—"

"Charlotte," Bayard said. "Hold him right there. If he moves, shoot him in the legs. I'll come through the house by the back way. When I reach the gallery, I want you to hand me the shotgun. And quickly—"

There was a sound off in the shadows and Adam Chaney's voice said, "Gordon, you've got no chance. Drop your gun."

Gordon felt a swift panic, and also a bitterness he could not conceal.

"So you're in it too, Adam," Gordon said heavily. He turned his head slightly in the direction of Adam Chaney's voice. Now he saw the rancher, standing well out of danger should Charlotte cut loose with the scattergun.

"I'm in it now," Adam Chaney said. "When my sister's happiness is threatened, perhaps her very life, it changes the complexion of things considerably."

Bayard had recovered from his surprise at his brother-in-law's sudden appearance. "Keep him covered, Adam. I'll get up behind him and get his gun. Charlotte, you get back in the house."

"I will not move until that man is off our property," Charlotte cried. "I won't have him around. He—he said some insulting things to me. He called my treasures—" she seemed to have a hard time getting the word out—"he called them junk."

"Very well," Bayard said. "Stay where you are then, Charlotte. Gordon, I suppose you can see you have no chance at all."

"So it seems."

"Adam, if he doesn't surrender his weapon I suggest you shoot him in the spine. Just above the waist is the spot. I've heard that a bullet there will result in instant paralysis."

Gordon dropped his gun. With a small cry of triumph Bayard came in behind him and scooped it up.

Chaney said, "Have you got a horse saddled, Roland?"

"No, but it won't take me long— Why do I need a horse? MacLane and his men should be here any minute. I sent Billy—"

"MacLane pulled out of town. He went back to Crazy Moon. I suggest we take our young friend to Seventy-Seven. Let Rin Orland deal with him. After all, why should you have blood on your hands? It's what you pay the man for."

Roland Bayard said nothing for a moment; he stared across the yard at his brother-in-law who stood in the deep shadows of a poplar. "Are you backing me up in this, Adam?"

"Why shouldn't I? After all, as I told you my sister's happiness—"

"Well, there have been times—" Bayard broke off. "Very well. I'll saddle a horse."

Bayard moved quickly around the house, his boots echoing hollowly on the hard-packed drive.

"Charlotte," Chaney said. "Please get back in the house."

"I will not budge."

Chaney sighed. "Guess I'll miss the supper tonight. But thanks for inviting me."

"There'll be other times, Adam. I—I suggest you have Mr. Orland escort Gordon out of the country. If he tries to return to spread his lies he should be horsewhipped."

Gordon felt a drop of sweat break across the bridge of his nose. He stood tensely. Charlotte still held the shotgun. She had not shifted the weapon. It still covered him. As Bayard had said earlier in his fright, one blast from that gun could cut a man to ribbons.

"I just never figured you'd do this, Adam," Gordon said.

"You had your chances. Lord knows I did my best to get you to leave the country. But I don't blame you for being bitter."

Bayard appeared riding a Morgan, leading Gordon's tired black. "I suggest a little precaution with this slippery gentleman," Bayard said. He rode close and dropped the noose of a saddle rope over Gordon's head, drawing it tight around the throat. "Now, my cocky friend, if you try and escape you'll have a broken neck for your trouble."

"It would be quick and painless," Adam Chaney said. "A lot more painless, maybe, than what Orland will do to him."

Bayard forced Gordon to mount. In a moment Chaney

rode up on the horse he evidently had left back in the trees.

"Charlotte," Bayard told his wife, "I want you to carefully let down the hammers of that weapon. I repeat, carefully. I don't ever want you to handle it again. A very dangerous weapon."

"Good thing I handled it tonight," she said. "I saved your hide, Roland."

"Yes—ahem—I suppose you did."

"I'd have helped you, Roland," Chaney said. "Even if Charlotte wasn't here. You know I would."

Bayard looked around. "Yes, I suppose so."

"I'll wait here until you're gone," Charlotte said firmly. "I will not budge until then."

They rode out of the yard and when they passed from the shelter of the trees the moon seemed to break out of dark clouds. Gordon eyed Bayard riding on his left. He felt that before this night was out he was going to kill Roland Bayard.

They rode for a mile and then Adam Chaney said, "I think a change of plan is in order."

Bayard reined in and Gordon hauled Spades to a halt because the pressure of the rope at his neck was suddenly intensified.

"Change of plan?" Bayard said. "What does that mean, Adam?"

"We'll go to my place instead of Seventy-Seven," Adam Chaney said. "There's something there I think Gordon should see."

There was a moment's silence from Bayard. "The Bible," he said hoarsely. "You mean the Bible."

Bayard rose in the stirrups and for a moment Gordon thought he would draw his gun and shoot Adam Chaney. But then Gordon saw a flicker of moonlight on metal. Chaney held a gun pointed at Bayard.

Bayard said, "You better stop and consider which side of the fence the gold mine is on."

"I've never taken one dollar from you, Roland, and you know it. Whatever I've gained has been with my own money. I learned some things about you before I came out here. I moved here to be near my sister. If you faced disaster I wanted to be on hand to protect her."

"Damned noble," Bayard said. He tried to appear as if he didn't care, but Gordon detected a note of panic in his voice. Bayard looked back at the lights of Table Rock glowing against the sky.

"If you're wondering if Halleck will bring help, forget it. I doubt if Billy Halleck is going to do you much good tonight," Chaney said. "I was on my way to your place for supper when Halleck appeared in your landau, driving too recklessly for safety. I rode after him and asked if there was trouble at your place. He told me. I ordered him back and he pulled a gun. I was a little quicker. He was pretty sick when I left him. I think his right arm is shattered."

Gordon had lifted the noose from his neck. He threw it to the ground. Bayard said nothing. Mechanically he drew in the rope and coiled it around the horn so his horse wouldn't trip on the dragging end.

"Shattered arm or not," Bayard said, "Halleck will get to MacLane. Billy is loyal. Which is more than I can say for my wife's own brother."

"I told you. MacLane and his men had already pulled out before I left."

Gordon said, "I don't feel dressed these days without a gun, Adam."

"Take Roland's. He won't object."

Gordon pushed Spades over against Bayard's horse. His hand went under Bayard's coat and brought out the revolver. Bayard cursed softly, but made no move toward Gordon for Chaney still held him covered.

"Reckon I figured you wrong, Adam," Gordon said. "I'm sorry."

"My sister was under an emotional strain. And she held a shotgun. And— Well, I couldn't chance her getting hurt. If I jumped Roland at the house there was no telling what might have happened."

Chaney ordered his brother-in-law to take the lead so they could watch him. They moved at a lope to Chaney's Double XX.

"I acted the fool with Roland," Gordon said. "I seen a note he left for Charlotte and the handwritin' didn't match up with the holdup note—"

"You'll have your answer when I show you the Bible. Roland gave it to me when he and Charlotte were married."

In Chaney's two-room shack a lamp was lighted on a shelf beside the stove. The Bible was taken from a hiding

124

place under the floor. Chaney blew off dust. It was a large book held together by a thick brass clasp. Chaney produced a key and unlocked it. Bayard, his face graying, looked on silently.

On the flyleaf of the Bible Chaney opened on the table Gordon read:

Julesburg, January 10, 1864

Adam—May this book remind you always of my sacred love for your sister, and assure you that it will last a lifetime.

Your brother-in-law

Roland

"I do love her," Bayard said. "I still do. And this persecution—"

Gordon stared at him. Then he looked down at the writing in the flyleaf again. He didn't need to compare the handwriting with that of the note. He felt empty. It had been such a long search. It had cost so much.

"This isn't anything like the way Roland writes now," Gordon said to Chaney.

"He gave me this Bible a few months before the robbery," Chaney said. "When he learned someway your father had kept that holdup note, Roland must have realized his mistake, changed his handwriting to cover up."

"When pa come here last year—" Gordon eyed Bayard. "You was scared pa had come to get you."

"I—I wasn't sure," Bayard said. "Look, I've made mistakes. Adam here has kept this Bible hanging over my head. I didn't think about the Bible until he showed up here. But I was already in too deep. I couldn't sell Seventy-Seven because Rin Orland had a taste of real money for the first time in his life. I couldn't control him. In fact, I'm afraid of the man."

"That's like having a mountain lion at the end of a short rope. You asked for it, Roland." Chaney closed the Bible. "Roland ransacked this place more than once, looking for this. Eh, Roland?"

Bayard said nothing.

"I sometimes feel," Chaney said, "that we both have protected Charlotte too much."

Bayard's heavy jowls quivered. "You're not suggesting that I be arrested for this—" he waved a hand at the

Bible—"this crime that was committed twenty years ago."

"That's up to Gordon."

Bayard wheeled on Gordon. "I'm still Opal's uncle! I reminded you of that fact once tonight. You send me to prison and she'll hate you to your dying day!"

There was a scuffing sound in the yard, then another. The three men in the shack stiffened. Gordon lifted a hand, ready to rush across the room and smash the lamp to the floor.

"He's in there with 'em." It was Billy Halleck's voice from outside.

Chaney said softly, "I should have made sure of Halleck."

Rin Orland said from outside, "Don't nobody move in there. Only you, Roland. Back out slow. Billy, keep your rifle on Conners."

Roland Bayard's stiffened face relaxed. "Good boy, Billy."

"I figured Chaney would head for his place, Mr. Bayard," Halleck said. "I got a bad arm but I rode for Seventy-Seven. I met Orland on his way into town. He figured the two of us could handle this job."

"The three of us," Bayard said. "Just let me get outside—"

Gordon shifted his gaze. He looked at Adam. Adam Chaney gave a slight nod of his head. Gordon was nearer the shelf that held the lamp than was Chaney. Without warning Gordon lunged for the lamp. Bayard's heavy body suddenly blocked him.

A gun crashed and Gordon felt a slicing pain along his right leg. As he fell back he saw the muzzle of a rifle poked through a side window, saw Halleck's face behind it.

Gordon found himself on the floor, a sudden numbness spreading along his right leg. Halleck fired again. The bullet chewed into the plank flooring. Gordon felt splinters cut into his neck.

His gun was out, cold in his hand. The revolver jarred him and he saw the spurt of orange-red flame leap from the muzzle of his gun toward the window. Halleck's face was no longer there.

Rolling over on his back Gordon saw Bayard and Chaney engaged in a hand-to-hand struggle for possession of Chaney's gun. They crashed against the stove at the far end of the room from Gordon. Bayard shouted.

The front door suddenly caved in. Rin Orland came piling into the room. His hat was gone. The dark face was cold. There was a beading of perspiration visible above his thin mustache. The black-handled gun was in his hand. He was lining it on Adam Chaney.

And then Gordon said, fighting pain and nausea, "Here, Orland."

Orland spun. His weapon and Gordon's made a thunderous crash. But Orland was already pitching over, firing. He fired into the floor, the reflex action emptying the gun into the planks. He crumpled and did not move.

It took a supreme effort for Gordon to gain his feet. He took two lurching steps, unable to see because of a fog. He realized he had been hit again. The leg pained and there seemed to be a white hot flame in his side.

He heard the gunshot, saw Adam Chaney collapse. He saw Roland Bayard spin, Chaney's gun in his hand.

The gun was spitting as it came around, but Gordon silenced it and the man behind it. Roland Bayard looked surprised and his knees slowly gave way under him.

He fell full length on the floor.

Chaney was not badly hit and he rode to town for a doctor. It seemed hours before a bunch of riders came whooping up from town, wanting to be in on the excitement. There was a wagon to handle the wounded. But there was only Gordon to take back to town alive.

And then there was Opal bending over Gordon in the wagon. He lay on blankets and he felt the jolt of the wagon.

"Your Uncle Roland," he said. "I—"

"Adam told me all about it, Gordon." Her voice shook. "It was your life or his. Adam is going to take Aunt Charlotte East to live with friends—"

"I'll be gone for a spell, Gordon," Chaney's voice came from the high seat of the wagon, beside the driver. "I need a partner. Someone young who can ride well and rope and likes the cow business."

Gordon couldn't answer. He felt Opal's tears on his face. He wanted to weep himself, but there seemed nothing left in him.

"But I'd prefer a married partner," Chaney said. "A

man who could build himself a house of whipsawed lumber. A man who could one day pay me back out of his profits."

Gordon couldn't remember much else. As they carried him into the doctor's house in Table Rock, a slender man wearing glasses pushed forward. He carried a notebook and pencil.

"Conners, I'm from the Table Rock *Enterprise*. Did either one of them say anything? After you shot them, I mean?"

"Only Orland. I think he said 'gun shy.' But I can't be sure."

THE END